CHALLENGER STORM
THE CURSE OF POSEIDON

AIRSHIP 27 PRODUCTIONS

CHALLENGER STORM—THE CURSE OF POSEIDON
© 2014 Don Gates

Published by Airship 27 Production
Airship27.com
Airship27Hangar.com

Interior & Cover illustrations © 2014 Michael W. Kaluta

Editor: Ron Fortier
Associate Editor: Ray Riethmeier
Promotions and Marketing Manager: Michael Vance
Production and design by Rob Davis.

ISBN-13: 978-0692266151 (Airship 27)
ISBN-10: 0692266151

Printed in the United States of America

10 9 8 7 6 5 4 3 2 1

CHALLENGER STORM
THE CURSE OF POSEIDON

DON GATES

AUTHOR'S NOTE: Within this novel the setting of Flying Platform #1, along with the characters of Commander Droste, Claire Lennartz, Damsky, Ellissen and the events mentioned in conjunction with them are from the motion picture version of Curt Siodmak's novel "F.P. 1 Does Not Reply" ("F.P. 1 Doesn't Answer." 1933). The film is now in the public domain, and since it offered an interesting solution for Storm and co.'s transatlantic flight dilemma (and the opportunity for a fun crossover), I just couldn't resist the chance to play in that particular sandbox for a few chapters. I hope I haven't offended any serious old-movie buffs by including these elements in my fictional world and hope readers will enjoy them and perhaps give the film a try if they are interested in more information.

– Don

PROLOGUE

T hough none of the people involved would ever know it, the thing that set the events in motion started at the beginning... the very start of everything.

From the moment of creation, the universe spread itself outward from its starting point and expanded, filling nothingness, making something where only emptiness had been before. Matter, energy, time, space... all flowed outward from the same cosmic fountainhead. The issue of whether the act was divinely planned or an unfathomable and random accident of science is debated, but nothing had suddenly become something and this could not be disputed.

The thing itself had been there at the moment it all started, created in that momentous split-second of chaotic birth. It was there as creation was let loose upon existence, and it fled the starting point with all other bits of cosmic debris that made up the fabric of reality. Hurtling through time and space, the thing was there as it passed through clouds of dust that would eventually become planets, past raging tempests of raw atomic energy that would calm and coalesce eventually into suns. The thing itself was barely fully-formed at first and spent countless centuries congealing and becoming whole, until at last it was a solid object. It flew onward in the frictionless void of space for unfathomable millennia on its trajectory, with no sentient mind of its own to wonder at its destination or the time that it would take to arrive there.

But arrive it eventually did, passing through half-formed constellations and untold solar systems until at last it reached what man would one day call the Milky Way. Its path brought it through this spinning river of stars to eventually cross a tiny cluster of planets in one of the system's outer-spiral arms. Finally, after an unthinkable period of time, it came close enough to an object whose gravitational pull was sufficiently strong to make it change its direction.

The thing—now a huge stony mass, leprous-green in color—had found itself pulled in toward Earth. It fell into a decaying orbit, and as it descended lower into the planet's atmosphere it began to fall apart: outer layers blistering and flaking off in the friction of its descent and of its own kinetic force. It fell, speeding toward its fated destination like an arrow from God....

Adeipho and his wife Philomela had watched the sun go down into the sea together from their spot on the hill. It had been a glorious sunset, and the day was settling down into a cool evening. The young loving couple had ceased their conversation soon after darkness had set in and had spent some time in silence, just enjoying the sounds of the waves lapping at the shore in the distance. Finally, Adeipho put his hand gently on his wife's smooth shoulder above the hem of her toga; she turned to him and smiled. It was time for them to go home.

The couple held hands as they made their way down the slope of the hill and to the road that wound down toward their seaside city. As they walked they conversed in low tones and they gazed ahead, past where the road curved and to the docks beyond as a myriad of sailing vessels and cargo ships bobbed up and down on the waves, their multitude of sails shining white in the early moonlight and the torches and lanterns of the wharf like squadrons of fireflies.

"Look at all those ships," Philomela had said to her husband in their musical native tongue. "They are bound for so many places: Crete, Troy, Athens and beyond…. It is such an exciting time now that our island-city has opened its ports and begun trading with the outside world." Concern clouded the contented smile on her face. "Don't you feel as though you are missing out on adventure at such a young age?" she asked him. "Instead of visiting other lands, you have tied yourself at home to our little grove of trees… and to me. Do you think you will ever miss that freedom, that adventure?"

Adeipho stopped and turned to look at his bride with nothing but tenderness in his heart. "I have all the adventure I will ever need, and freedom as well. You have given me wings," he said. He reached out and stroked her cheek gently, and she smiled up at him.

Suddenly Philomela's eyes flicked upward from his gaze, and they focused over Adeipho's head and into the night sky out above the dark ocean. "Oh…" she said, voice lost in wonder.

Adeipho turned to look as well, and he saw what it was that had awed his wife: high in the sky, past the dark curtains of clouds that been clumped in the distance, a glow was flickering and growing. The light was feeble at first but was now moving slowly across the heavens, becoming stronger as it moved in their direction. It looked as though the sun was rising beyond the clouds, even though it had only been dark for a little over an hour.

Something felt very wrong.

"I want to go home," Philomela said in a small voice, and her husband nodded. Something strange was happening in the sky, and the couple wanted to be near the safety of their city and its temples, their families and neighbors.

They started to jog toward the city, now less than a kilometer away from them. They never reached it.

The light in the sky was moving much faster than either of them could know, faster than they ever thought possible. There was a sound like thunder and from the dark clouds a streak of light fell faster than their eyes could follow. It struck their beloved city in a park not too far away from the tiny metropolis' center, and with its impact the land itself seemed to leap into the air. A stunning, stone-crushing shockwave spread outward, and after that a massive firestorm rippled from the point of the meteor strike. It engulfed houses, markets, streets…. Anyone or anything that was still standing now was torn, pulverized, and engulfed in flame. The sea broke out into a rolling boil almost instantly, and a massive tremor had begun in the ground.

Adeipho and Philomela had been hurled to the ground when the impact had occurred, and now the young farmer shakily helped his wife to her feet. There was no time for questions though; no time for mourning… there was only time to flee. They turned and ran, hand in hand and panicking, as massive cracks and fissures sprang up around them and spread outward all through the island. It was as though a massive plate had been struck in the middle and was shattering in slow motion, falling apart from its center. Simultaneously, the boiling sea was rushing upward, rolling over the land. The pieces of their fragmented island were sinking now, and Adeipho and Philomela ran in a panic for whatever land would support them the longest before being swallowed by the waves.

Fast as the couple's fear could carry them, however, the apocalypse that had struck their island home was much faster: a deep chasm suddenly appeared beneath Philomela's running feet and she slipped into it with a cry of helpless terror. Adeipho's grip on her hand was firm, and the sudden force of his wife's falling yanked him from his feet and flat onto his stomach there at the edge of the sudden gap.

Wide-eyed, Philomela struggled in the suddenly-formed abyss and dangled from Adeipho's gripping hand. She managed to swing her other arm up to grip her husband's forearm, and he too managed to reach down with his free hand to grip her other arm.

She looked up, eyes locking with those of Adeipho, and for a tiny, unspoken moment the two communicated their love stronger than they ever had before. It was a final moment, they knew, before death would claim them. Then, the edge upon which Adeipho was lying crumbled and the couple fell, still grasping each other, spiraling downward into the crack in the earth and the water that was rushing in now to fill it.

The waves continued their furious onslaught, and the island's fragments became smaller and smaller, crumbling into the boiling sea that was claiming it, finishing the job that the thing from the sky had started. The burning trees were eventually extinguished by the climbing waves, the stones of the ruined buildings swept and tumbled from the ground, the bones of the citizens hidden by the foaming sheet of the sea....

When the sun again rose upon the Aegean Sea the following morning, there was one less jewel of green on its expanse of deep blue. The island was simply no longer there. It had been erased from the face of the world by the strange meteor, and only a few people were left alive to tell of the curse that they believed had claimed it.

CHAPTER 1:
OUT OF THE FOG

ast of Athens, Greece, in the Aegean Sea, the freighter *Arapaho* chugged along at a leisurely pace. The boat was a bit rusty and beaten-up, but the old craft was tough as nails and praised by her crew for its durability. Her screws beat the black water into a milky froth in the quiet and still moonlit night as she headed south between Andros and Chios, two of the larger islands in the landmass-studded expanse of sea.

Deep in thought, young Robert Culver smoked a cigarette and gazed from the ship's port-side railing. The *Arapaho*'s passage had been quiet, completely free of anything remotely exciting or eventful. Culver, twenty years old and full of youthful fire, had absolutely hated every minute of it. He had joined the crew of the cargo steamer a year earlier, hoping to find adventure and excitement, to see the world and experience things that he had only daydreamed about in his humdrum upbringing in Arizona. Instead of these adventurous sights and experiences, he had seen a lot of the mattress in his bunk, and he had seen a lot of water, and that was about it. He regretted his decision now that he had spent so much uneventful and mind-numbingly boring time at sea but there was no turning back now. It would be weeks before the ship would draw into a port in the United States, weeks of the torturous agony of nothingness until he could get off the boat and go back to his normal life of daydreams and reading dog-eared copies of "*Adventure*" and whatever else he could get his hands on that featured exciting escapades in far-off lands. He wondered if he would ever be able to enjoy them again, after having such banal "adventures" of his own.

Bitterly, Culver took another drag from his cigarette and gazed out to sea. It was a perfect, clear evening. Not too warm, not a cloud in the sky, and the sea as calm and smooth as a sheet of glass. To some it would have been idyllic; to Culver, it was hellish.

In the boat behind him, someone shouted something in Greek, and then laughed as others joined in. The locals who had signed on to the voyage were having a great time, evidently, and Culver smiled faintly to himself. At least someone is enjoying themselves tonight, he thought.

Maybe he would join them in a game of cards or something, anything to alleviate the tedium and monotony he felt.

He straightened from the railing and began to turn away when something in the distance caught his eye: a faint patch of mist had sprouted from the sea, and it clung oddly to the water. As Culver gazed at it he suddenly became aware that not only was the mist thickening and spreading, but the focal point of the mist was also moving toward the *Arapaho*. Soon, the paths of the ship and the mist, which had rapidly become a dense fog, would intersect. Something about that swirling patch of fog worried the young sailor.

Culver went inside and climbed the steps to the upper-deck and wheelhouse. Captain Westernook himself, a weathered and greying man, was at the wheel, aged eyes peering at the sea ahead of the ship's bow.

"Cap'n," started Culver, "there's… there's something out there. There's a weird patch of fog moving toward us, sir, from the east. It's headin' right for us."

Westernook looked over his shoulder at the normally quiet seaman, his eye regarding him suspiciously. "Fog? The devil, man. There's not a cloud in the sky for miles, and it isn't the weather for it. You're drunk." At this, Westernook's first mate, Dennison, broke out in laughter.

Culver, constantly the butt of jokes on board the *Arapaho*, bristled at this but did his best to maintain his composure. "I'm serious, sir," he said. Then, from the corner of his eye he realized it was visible now through one of the wheelhouse's portholes. "There," he said, pointing. "It's shifted its course again and still heading this way." Westernook followed Culver's pointing finger and looked.

The weird mist had indeed changed its heading: it was now coming directly for them, as though matching their speed, leading them as a marksman would lead his running prey through the sights of his rifle.

Westernook stared thoughtfully for a moment. "Mr. Dennison, take the wheel," the captain finally commanded, and then he left the bridge after motioning for Culver to follow him.

By the time the two men had emerged out onto the deck of the freighter, the fog had converged with the steamer, and the strange mist had fully enveloped the entire *Arapaho*. The full moon, so brightly illuminating just minutes before, had become muted, nearly obscured by the strange billowing mist. Below the railing, Westernook and Culver could just barely make out the waves. The captain cursed, and then returned to the steamer's bridge to order a full-stop from the engine room. The engine order telegraph bells rang out, and in moments the *Arapaho* slowed then stopped altogether to drift on the unseen black water. There was quiet now, suddenly, and the scene was eerie without the comforting throb of the ship's engines.

Aroused by the sudden change, the crew began to file out from within the ship and onto the deck. Grunting complaints mingled with sarcastic responses, and Culver shared the mirth with his fellows until he noticed the Greek sailors among them. They were not laughing; instead, they gazed out at the fog and seemed to try to pierce it with their hunted-looking eyes. At last, a murmured phrase began to escape their lips, and they became more and more pale as they discussed among themselves.

Captain Westernook, like most of his crew, did not speak Greek. "Stalfos, what are they on about?" he asked his chief translator.

Stalfos, a skeletal-looking Greek, did not look as pale as the rest of the Greeks on the boat did, but looked oddly concerned himself.

"A local legend, Cap'n... a superstition. A curse, they speak of... the curse of Poseidon. Something very old about the wrath of the gods, about stealing the ships of trespassers and anyone who comes through the sea without appeasing them. They say the sea is angry again... that it claims its own, and it'll strike out at anyone, even those on land, who take from the sea or tread upon it without permission."

"Poppycock," replied the bearded captain. "Tell them to pull themselves together or..."

"Ice!" someone called out, interrupting Westernook's admonition. "We've got ice astern!"

The shout came from the rear of the boat. Westernook hurried to the stern, fully prepared to scold the sailor who had shouted nonsense about ice. He stopped dead in his tracks, however, as he gazed down from the railing and saw that ice had indeed formed around the ship. Everywhere the sailors looked they found the *Arapaho* was embedded in thick, darkly-glittering crystals of ice, and the ship's silent propellers were now encased in slabs of the white stuff, preventing movement.

"What the...?" Westernook's jaw was slack, and he nearly dropped his pipe overboard in his bewildered state. Somehow, the *Arapaho* had become gripped by an iceberg there in the warm Mediterranean waters off the coast of Greece.

Suddenly, the ship's lights went out and the *Arapaho* was plunged into dimly-lit darkness, the moonlight barely struggling to get through the intense and strange fog. Something was afoot, and superstition was running wild, even within the captain's logical mind.

The Greek sailors began talking wildly in their native language. "Shut that lot up!" the captain shouted at Stalfos, then began to formulate orders. Crews would be lowered in the lifeboats, and they would hack away at the strange ice with their hatchets and fire-axes until the boat was free. Then, Westernook planned, they would run like a bat out of hell toward shore: the nearness to land would be comforting for the sailors, including the old captain, who had seen a lot of strange things at sea but none so weird as these events.

Captain Westernook opened his mouth to give out his orders. He would never say those words.

From the dark waves around the boat came a series of loud splashes; dimly-seen forms seemed to erupt from the water and sail through the air. Each shape landed on the deck of the *Arapaho* with a resounding thump and they promptly proceeded to uncoil themselves. There was instant chaos as the sailors tried to flee the shapes: through the mist and darkness the shapes looked like the dim, black outlines of men but the shapes were exaggerated, threatening. Each man-shape was oversized with thick limbs, torso and head. The shoulders of the invading shapes were covered in thorny spikes, and each threatening and dimly-seen form brandished an odd spear-like weapon at the ship's crew.

In the confusion and sudden terror, the sailors found themselves herded and corralled together near the front of the ship. Groups of the strange humanoid shapes were closing in from the *Arapaho*'s bow and stern around them, and the captives found themselves even more confused and frightened as impossibly-white beams of light erupted from the attacking shapes' heads, blinding them. The sailors were all hardened men, used to rough ports and fights for survival, but they knew they were outclassed by the invaders from the sea: none had ever encountered enemies this weird and terrifying.

"What's the meaning of this?" Westernook roared as he stepped to the front of the captives. He glared at the newcomers toward the ship's bow as defiantly as he could, but had to shield his eyes from the glare of the multiple lights. In response to his bellowed demand, a figure detached itself from the invading shapes in the mist. It was hulking and taller than the other invaders and it towered over the aged captain of the *Arapaho*, pinning him in the inhumanly cold and bright light streaming from its head. The deck trembled slightly with each footstep that the shape took. Behind the light, the head of the chief-invader was adorned with the spiky suggestion of a crown.

The voice of the leader was cold and icy, and it reverberated through the mist in unearthly tones. "You have trespassed upon my kingdom, Captain. You have thereby forfeited your vessel and the lives of yourself and your crew. These things all belong now to me."

Westernook balled a fist and stepped forward, enraged. "Who the hell do you think you are?" He started to swing.

The punch that struck instead came from the towering leader and it was so swift it seemed almost without motion. It slugged into Westernook's abdomen like a sledgehammer and he fell over backward and doubled up in agony. The crew tensed, but their anger was met by the bristling threat of the invaders' weapons.

"I am Poseidon," the leader intoned, "the lord of these waters, and your new master." He raised his head and the lights from his fellows caught his skin, reflecting the sheen of black metal. "Bow before me!" he commanded the sailors.

Robert Culver crouched alone and hidden near the bow, covered in a cold sweat. He gripped a Luger pistol in his slick palms; like the other sailors, he kept a weapon in case of any trouble, although there had been no need for it... not before now. Culver had kept the pistol on him at all times, however, and found himself the only sailor to be armed at the moment. The way he looked at it, he could be the crew's only hope for salvation. He was scared, though, and he found it hard to breathe. With an effort, he swallowed hard and made up his mind: he'd take out the leader of the mysterious attackers, deflating their morale or, he hoped, startling them long enough for the crew to overtake them.

Culver said a prayer then sprang from his crouch and rounded the bow, his Luger squarely leveled and aimed at the back of the leader's head. His hand shook, but he pulled the trigger.

The roar of the shot mixed with a metallic plink-sound of a ricochet, but the leader did not go down. The attackers at the bow spun around as one and their lights stabbed at Culver, who began to pull the Luger's trigger for a second shot.

But there were no further shots fired from Culver's pistol.

A series of rapid, sharp hisses—like someone sucking their teeth loudly—were heard from the spear-like weapons of the mysterious mist-shrouded shapes. One, two… four times something glittery struck Culver in the chest, and bloody gouts erupted from his back. He jumped back and struck the railing before he flipped over it and into the black water below.

The hostages stared in dumb horror as the brave runt of the *Arapaho*'s crew was cut down by the strange attackers from the mist. The killers turned back toward the crew and threatened them again with their weapons.

"Let his death serve as a warning to you all… to anyone who would dare challenge the rule of Poseidon over this sea." The evil, booming voice of the leader seemed to mock the sailors who had been unable to act in the face of their friend's death. They silently mourned the murder of their young crewmate even as they began to realize something strange: the *Arapaho*, though partially encased and crippled by the strange ice, had begun to move. The motion was too fast for simple drifting, the ship was actually *moving* ahead into the darkness under a mysterious outer-influence.

The steamer and its crew quietly sailed onward into the eerie mist, which seemed to swallow them like the mythical Kraken of legend. A short time later, the weird fog lifted and cleared. In the mist's absence there was no trace of the *Arapaho*'s existence left behind, save for a few pieces of the strange ice and the lonely floating body of young Robert Culver.

CHAPTER 2:
A FRIEND IN NEED

The Wedell-Williams speed-plane, a rare Model 44, began its descent over Miami. Aeronautic enthusiasts on the ground who spotted the aircraft shielded their eyes against the early-morning sun to get a better view of the craft as it passed over them. The plane was striking: it was painted a bright canary-yellow, and on the port side of its fuselage was a stylized art-deco depiction of a running hunting-hound painted in bright and shining silver. It gleamed in the clear, bright air of the Florida morning. The craft was a curiosity: only a few Model 44's were ever built and they were notable for competing in several air-races. This particular Model 44 had never flown in any competitions, and its owner and pilot had commissioned the building of the craft for themselves directly from the manufacturer.

The plane flew southeast, over the glittering jewel of the city proper and toward the blue ribbon of Biscayne Bay. Below it, the beaches and tourists and grand hotels passed serenely as the plane arrowed toward its destination. Finally, near the southernmost mouth of the bay, the yellow and silver Wedell-Williams fell into a holding-circle. The pilot requested clearance to land at the sprawling private airfield and compound below: a collection of hangars, workshops, and assorted buildings arranged in a semi-circle that faced the azure waters beyond.

The control tower soon gave clearance, and the Wedell-Williams began its descent, skimming in finally in a graceful landing at the smaller of the compound's runways. The yellow speed-plane taxied to a nearby hangar where a small group of coverall-clad mechanics was waiting.

The engine was killed and the prop ceased its spinning. The mechanics, who all wore grins and were obviously glad to see the arrival, advanced on the plane. From the opening cockpit the pilot emerged: an athletic and long-legged female clad in a leather jacket and jodhpur pants. Removing her leather flight helmet and goggles, she shook out a cascading mane of jet-black hair and smiled at the mechanics.

"Hello, boys," she said in a throaty yet feminine voice. "Is Cliff around?"

Outside of the compound's fence, in a far corner of the property, a pair of dark-clothed men watched the scene from their hidden perch in a tree with high-powered binoculars. They had waited for days now for the yellow speed-plane to arrive. As they had watched it descend onto the runway, their previous lethargy gave way to relief. "Yeah, that's the broad, all right," said the taller of the men as he watched the aviatrix climb from her ship. "Our dope in the glasses was right to say she'd come here… she's goin' in now."

"Geez, I'm glad that part's over with," the shorter man said. He was mopping his forehead repeatedly with a handkerchief; as he started to climb down from the tree, a passerby (if there were any) would have noticed the huge crescents of sweat-stains beneath his arms. The Florida heat was disagreeing with him. "I'll make the call," he said to his companion from the ground. He was eager to get in out of the swelter. The taller man remained in the tree and continued to watch the complex beyond the fence with interest; he grunted a reply as the other walked to their parked car, hidden across the road behind a clump of bushes.

The airfield and the surrounding compound were home to a brain-trust, an assorted collection of scientists, engineers, mechanics, and industrial designers that had been brought together for one common goal: the betterment of mankind through advancements in technology. The Miami Aerodrome Research and Development Laboratories (MARDL for short) was a nearly-constant hive-like buzz of work, always with an eye on the future as it strove toward its utopian goals. However, the MARDL complex was also the home base to a group of troubleshooters: skilled specialists, ragtag thrill-seekers and adventuring misfits, all geared toward helping people in need and punishing the guilty and oppressive… not for glory or for payment of any kind, but simply because it was the right thing to do.

The man responsible for this organization and its astounding members and achievements was sitting behind a huge mahogany desk in his private office, which was located in the main building: a combination of control tower and administration structure. The room around him was cluttered with books, maps, charts, files, reports, and other miscellanea while a huge antique globe rested beside the desk. The man behind the desk was athletic but trim and not at all bulky, built like a marathon runner at the peak of his development, and he seemed to radiate a sense of quiet energy. He seemed like a spring that was coiled and waiting for a hair-trigger release to send it into action. His eyes, a steely blue-grey, were set in a face that could almost be called handsome. The face, however, had been marred some time ago by three long scars running down the left side, from the hairline down to the jaw, and one scar ran even further and down the man's neck.

The owner of the face was Clifton Storm... the world called him "Challenger."

Years ago, Storm had been a shallow and spoiled youth living off the fortune that his benevolent parents had amassed. He had been away from home on one of his jaunts of debauchery when they had been killed in an automobile accident. On his way back to attend to his parents' funeral and financial affairs his plane was caught in a freak ice-storm over the Smoky Mountains and crashed. All the other passengers were killed but Clifton Storm alone was spared, save for the scarring facial injury. Left alone in the mountains to die, Storm had experienced an epiphany and decided that his life had been meaningless and empty up to that point. He decided that he had been left alive for a special reason and he went on to spend every waking moment helping his fellow man and training himself for his new role as guardian of the innocent.

From college, where he excelled in a wide variety of subjects, he had embarked on a globe-spanning trip of self-discovery during which he had learned and honed an array of martial and combative skills. He had returned, finally, to his beloved city of Miami where he built the Miami Aerodrome Research and Development Laboratories using his enormous family-fortune. From this base of operations, Storm had undertaken high-profile missions of danger and derring-do and the media had eaten up his exploits with a spoon. They had given him the nickname "Challenger" due to his success in the face of the odds that he and his troubleshooters had faced while on their adventures.

In his office, Storm ran a hand through his black hair and resumed his perusal of the folder in front of him. It was a collection of analyses, reports, and findings concerning an unusual mineral that had been brought back with his group when they returned from a previous adventure on the tiny island-nation of La Isla de Sangre. When manipulated by electrical currents, the stuff—called Skyrock—exhibited some peculiar anti-gravity qualities; Storm's staff of scientists had been experimenting on the Skyrock since they brought a quantity back with them a month previous. A myriad of hypothetical uses and inventions utilizing the material were running through the adventurer's mind....

Storm's reverie was broken by the buzz of his intercom. He reached out

Clifton Storm...the world called him "Challenger."

to toggle the talk button only to realize that the intercom wasn't visible on his desk, only the small mountain of desk-clutter which he began digging through. The intercom buzzed again somewhere as he dug through the pile in search of it, and papers and books sluiced off the messy desk as he continued searching for the device. Suddenly, the buzzing stopped. As Storm kept searching for the missing intercom there were footsteps outside his closed door, followed by a polite knocking.

"Come in," Storm answered, still absorbed in the search through the office-mess.

The door swung open and Marie Larue, Storm's secretary, walked in. The full-figured redhead watched her boss search in vain for his intercom for a moment then she went directly to a small and haphazardly piled heap of books in the corner. She patted Storm's Boston terrier, Buddy, on the head as she walked past him. Reaching into the pile of books, she withdrew the buried intercom box and handed it to her sheepishly-smiling boss who thanked her. Marie cleared her throat daintily as he cleared a space for the intercom on his desk and set it down.

He looked up at her. "Yes?"

"You have a visitor: Diana St. Clair," she replied, hands behind her back.

"Oh… Diana. Wonder what she's here for." Storm scratched the back of his head. "Send her in please, Marie."

The secretary left and returned a moment later with the tall aviatrix who had recently landed in the yellow plane. As Storm showed Diana to a seat (clearing a file folder out of it first), Marie left the room, closing the door behind her.

Storm offered his guest a cup of Cuban coffee from the urn at the side of the room and sat back down behind his desk. He regarded the woman before him; it had been a while since he last saw Diana St. Clair. She was one of his troubleshooters, a debutante and society girl who found the call to adventure a little too hard to ignore; Diana thus joined Storm's crew of do-gooders for the excitement that her high-class life of luxury was missing. Besides being a pilot of respectable skill, she also was an extremely skilled crack-shot whose weapon of choice was a modified long-range hunting rifle, and she was able to apply those hobbies to suit the needs of Storm's adventures.

"Geez, Cliff," Diana said as she took the coffee cup and gazed around the cluttered office. "This place is still as much a rat's nest as the last time I saw it."

He scoffed. "No need to be rude, Diana. I prefer the phrase 'lived-in,'" he responded with a smile.

"Yeah, 'lived-in' is right... I'll bet there are all kinds of things living in here," she teased.

Storm laughed. "All right now... I know you didn't just drop in to give me a hard time about house-keeping... I have Marie for that," he gestured toward the door. "Something must be up."

"There is," Diana said, leaning back in her chair and crossing her legs. "That's why I'm here."

Storm raised an eyebrow quizzically.

"Has the Aegean Sea come to your attention lately?" Diana continued. "Or more specifically, the weird things that have been going on there?"

Storm shook his head. MARDL received constant and countless updates about events occurring all around the world: war-zones, hot-spots of conflict, epidemics, disasters both man-made and natural, tense political situations... any situation that may warrant Storm and his troubleshooting collective's interest. These were reported by an affiliated network of journalists and freelance sources, whose telephone calls, radio messages, or telegraphs were transcribed by a team of specialists in a special room of the compound. These communication staff-members would then send them to Storm via a pneumatic tube-system, and thus Storm would be apprised of global situations as fast as most news agencies, if not faster in some cases. He had been unaware, however, of any scenario specifically located within the blue and green waters of the Aegean.

"No, huh?" Diana shrugged her shoulders. "I figured as much... I've been speculating myself about a bit of a press blackout over there. Maybe someone doesn't want word of what's happening there to leak out into the rest of the world."

"And that is...?" Storm prodded her.

Diana's eyes riveted Storm's gaze with their sapphire-like intensity. "In the past six months, ten different ships have disappeared from the waters of the Aegean. Cargo ships, mostly, hauling steel and other building materials. But two of the ships were different: one was a passenger ship carrying a load of workers to some kind of big construction job in Crete... that was the second boat to disappear. Then there was the first ship to go missing... a science vessel carrying an expedition team of research scientists and undersea explorers headed up by Roderick Manton...."

"Now, that one I've heard about," Storm interrupted. "Manton was some kind of big-wig in the field of oceanography. I've got one of his books about the mystery of the Sargasso Sea. I'd heard he disappeared with a team of his and that they were on a world-wide trip to study underwater volcanic activity, but I'm afraid I don't know any more details beyond that."

Diana nodded. "The most recent stop on their trip had been a survey site near Pompeii. After that, they sailed off into the sunset and were never heard from again."

Storm frowned and held his chin in his hand as he gazed into space past Diana. He was deep in thought, and his blue-grey eyes had gone dark. "All these ships," he said slowly, "they just vanished into thin air?"

"Most of them," the adventurous society-girl said. "A small fishing boat chanced to be near one of the ship's routes and they spotted some odd fog in the vicinity once, but nothing too bizarre beyond that. But there is a bit more, something I didn't mention to you before now."

"What's that?"

The comely aviatrix smiled: "I know you're going to love this one. The locals claim these boats are victims of a curse laid upon the sea by the Greek god Poseidon himself."

Storm leaned back in his chair as his eyebrows rose in interest. He was silent as he thought over the situation over, particularly with the ethereal new angle that Diana had revealed to him. Finally, he leaned forward again and folded his hands on his desk.

"Say, Diana..." he said quizzically. "If this is all so hush-hush and secret, then how did you come by this information yourself?"

Diana St. Clair's smile remained, but the look in her eyes softened a little suddenly. "Because Herbert Chalmers was on that science vessel... the first one that disappeared."

Storm's face froze. "Oh no... I'm sorry to hear that, Diana," he said. He was wholly unprepared for this new angle to the tale.

Herbert Chalmers had been a MARDL scientist since the very beginning of Storm's organization. He was a geologist, and when he'd received an offer to work with a prestigious board of scientists with a well-known New England university, Storm had let Chalmers go from his team with his blessing, telling the young scientist that there would always be room for him at MARDL in the future.

On an even more personal note, however, was Chalmers' relationship with Diana St. Clair, and the way Storm had felt about it. The bookish earth-scientist and the adventuress had been involved romantically for quite a while, but it hadn't been favorable to Storm. At one time he had harbored feelings for Diana himself, a secret affection that he had never revealed to her, and he wondered for a while if he had held any dislike of Chalmers. Chalmers had been a genuinely nice guy, though, and Storm had realized that it wasn't Chalmers' fault that he had missed his chance with Diana, but because of his own relentless pursuit of justice and betterment and the ways that he could apply himself to help others. His pursuits had taken his time and energy and he had found himself alone and he never tried to change his situation. He hadn't taken any chances with Diana, and Herbert Chalmers had stepped in and swept her off her feet while Storm had pined for her inside like a lovesick high-schooler.

He thought he had let those feelings go some time ago, however, chalking it all up to a boyish crush, but sitting in the office with Diana he felt the stirring of those old feelings. In the meantime, Diana and Chalmers had broken up shortly before Chalmers had left MARDL. The split was amicable and the two had remained on good speaking terms, and Storm could now see the sadness in her eyes was concern for her old flame. Storm's interest in this case was now doubled because of Diana's connection with Chalmers, as well as his own concern for his friends and for the crews of the missing vessels.

"Herbert and I," she said, "we split up because his work had become more important to him than he and I were. I was okay with that, I guess… men like Herbert are more likely to use their minds better than their hearts. Even though we weren't a couple anymore we were close… closer than we had been before we broke up, actually. He had been excited to be on his new position, and I was happy for him. When his ship disappeared, I began investigating the circumstances. I did a bit of poking around there in Greece myself, but despite all my digging and snooping I haven't found the first sign of what happened to him, just this tale of ships and their disappearances." Diana paused, gathering her thoughts and emotions. "I have a feeling that whatever trouble he's been snagged by is big, Cliff… really big. I don't suppose…."

"I can be ready to go in an hour," he said. "How about you?"

CHAPTER 3:
THE CURSE STRIKES
AGAIN

At the moment Storm was agreeing to accompany Diana on her investigation, the small seaside village of Katsopolis, near Thessalonica in Greece, was quieting down for the evening. The Aegean Sea was seven hours ahead of Miami, and the sun would be setting over the azure-and-emerald stretch of the planet soon. Katsopolis was tucked away in a small northwestern corner of the Aegean and was a quiet and peaceful place. The little town was a small collection of single-level white brick and stucco dwellings; it was set back from the water on a slight rise of land, and between it and the beach were some low sand-dunes. On the beach the fishermen, tired and weather-beaten from the shining sun of the day, were beginning to haul in the last of their nets. Eels, blennies, gar, and a host of other types of fish struggled in the net as the fishermen smiled at the final haul.

Nine-year old Nikos ran down the dunes and out to where his father pulled in his net. It had been a good haul, and his father was readying the last of his baskets to be filled by his catch. Avram heard Nikos calling "Papa!" and turned to the boy. Smiling, he dropped his basket and hoisted the boy in his arms. He hadn't seen Nikos since the night before, since he had left for the beach and fishing early in the morning while he'd been asleep.

"Hello, Nikos!" he greeted the boy. "Look, we've got plenty of fish tonight. What luck, eh? We will have plenty of money from the market tomorrow."

Nikos nodded his eyes wide as he looked down at the bounty from the water. He had heard his parents talking about the fishing lately. It had been poor for a while in this area, and most of the people in Katsopolis thrived on what they could catch. The fish had seemed to disappear for a long time recently, and the beach had been nearly empty in the last few weeks as every day fewer fishermen returned to it. This day had indeed been prosperous, however, and the boy was looking forward to seeing the haggard look in his father's eyes lift with the promise of renewed luck.

"I want to help," Nikos offered.

Avram chuckled and set the boy down beside him. "Very well, then, you can help me gather up…"

Avram stopped abruptly. The beach trembled.

It was just for a moment and then was gone, but there had been a definite tremor beneath their feet. Nikos had been swayed, and Avram steadied him with a hand on his shoulder. "Easy, now," he said. Looking around, the pair saw the other fishermen were startled as well, and they too looked around them in confusion.

Suddenly, one of the fishermen bellowed something and pointed toward the sea, then turned and ran. Avram and Nikos followed his point and saw a startling vision. The water had receded from the beach an alarming distance, exposing some shallow-swimming fish that flopped on the exposed sand. Incredible as the sight of the outrushing tide was, it paled next to what they saw beyond it: the water was swelling. A blue-green wall seemed to be forming and surging forward toward the beach. The wave seemed to be gathering momentum, growing as it neared them. A sound like thunder was filling their ears and shaking their bones.…

Avram scooped his son up in his arms and raced back toward the dunes, the other panicking fishermen fleeing around them as well. Nikos shouted and Avram turned, seeing the onrushing wall of water at the corner of his vision. It was nearing their backs and about to overtake them, and he knew there was no way to outrun the wave.

"Hold your breath Nikos, and hold on to Papa!" he yelled. With that the water crashed around them, slamming the pair forward and off their feet with tremendous force. They were suddenly submerged.

The wave had been huge and had enveloped them in the rushing salt-water. After being thrust forward for a few moments Avram felt the forward momentum of the wave slow and reverse, and knew he and Nikos could be in danger of being sucked out to sea. Opening his eyes in the briny seawater, he blurrily saw they had been pushed past the dunes and there were a few paving stones here on the ground, loose but heavy. He reached down and grabbed the edge of one of these stones with his right hand while clutching Nikos with his left. As the water drew back to the beach the stone held, and eventually the father and son found themselves free of the wave.

Nikos coughed and sucked in air while Avram looked around. He could see the town was nearer, and the residents had come out in the streets to look around in fear and confusion. After scanning the faces in the crowd and failing to find his wife's, he looked around for his fellow fishermen. He could see only a few of them now, though, and he knew that some of them must have been taken by the wave's undercurrent.

All thoughts of recovery fled as another tremor shook the ground, deeper and longer this time, as the father and his son were getting to their feet. The crowd in the town felt it and they had trouble standing. A cry went up from the nearest clump of people and they turned and fled; a panic began to spread through the entire village crowd. Nikos and his father turned to see yet another huge wave building out in the Aegean, and once again they scrambled toward the buildings of Katsopolis and whatever shelter they could reach before the next wave hit.

Nikos could not run as fast as his father, so again Avram scooped the boy up in his arms. Ahead the streets and buildings of the village beckoned, but this time Avram knew they would not make it. Instead, he ran toward a tall tree that grew near the division where the grass became sand. The tree was tall and strong and towered over the village; if he could not make the climb to the top, at least maybe Nikos could....

Avram reached the tree with only moments to spare. This second wave was much larger than the first, and he knew what could happen, especially if another wave followed. He plucked the boy's hands from his shirt and lifted him into the lowest branches, straining on his tip-toes to reach him up to them.

The boy struggled. "No, Papa! No, stay with me!"

Avram's voice vibrated with fear, but he commanded it. "Nikos, you must grab on. No matter what, hold onto that tree! Climb when you can! Climb to the top!"

The scared boy started to protest again and ask about his mother, but the wave struck, slamming into the tree with tremendous force. The survival instinct kicked in and Nikos clutched at the branches around him, while Avram's arms encircled the trunk. The water rushed further inland this time, rushing through the streets of Katsopolis and catching the fleeing crowd in the street. Amid all the rushing of the water yet another, deeper tremor vibrated the ground. Another wave would be following this one, faster this time, and even larger.

The second wave receded and Avram choked out a final "Climb!" to Nikos, who moved upward through the tree branches. He ran then, away from Nikos and the hopeful safety of the tree and into the town. People gasped and floundered and ran everywhere, and in a moment of sick irony Avram remembered the fish he'd caught earlier, gasping on the beach for air.

As Avram's feet pounded on the slick paving stones beneath his feet, he called for his wife. Looking over his shoulder he saw yet another monstrous wave rising out in the water in the distance. He bolted forward up the streets, shiny with water, to the tiny house he shared with his son and wife. She stood there now in the doorway; she had been there all along and was just venturing out of their tiny home now. Avram ran to her and they threw their arms around each other just as the third wave hit, flooding the streets in a shower of water and foam and the screaming chorus of fear from those around them....

Nikos had clung to the strongest of the tree's uppermost branches and weathered the furious waves as they continued. He had lost sight of his father, of the entire town's people after the fourth wave, and there had been many more waves afterwards. The tree was strong and tall, and so even though the waves had remained high he had found himself above the worst of the water. Nikos wasn't sure how long he remained in the tree but it was dark before the cycle of tremors and tidal waves had stopped. When it did cease, it was abrupt: there was no gradual subsiding or dying down of the tremors and waves. It simply ended as though a switch had been thrown. It was after the sun went down that a dark stillness descended upon the ghost-town that had been Katsopolis.

Nikos remained in the tree. He was cold now even though he had dried out eventually, and he was scared. Here and there in the gloom, he could see where some of the village's weaker structures had collapsed beneath the onslaught of the waves; he could also see the shapes that he knew had to be the dead bodies of the townspeople. The thought of his mother and father lying there, cold and still somewhere in the streets, brought tears to his eyes and Nikos wept from his perch. What would he do now? What *could* he do now?

It was while he was looking down in sorrow that a light out on the water caught his eye.

He wiped his tears and realized there were more of them: six lights in all. Here and there, they dotted the nearby waves down by the shore and they were extremely bright as they swept the water back and forth. What were they? Nikos' fear and sadness was overcome by a strange sense of wonder, and he craned his head to see the lights better.

They were nearing the shore now, in the shallows of the beach, and in the glare of the lights he could now make out the hulking figures that were projecting them. He started to cry out but froze instead: something about the outlines of the figures, their shape, made him hesitate. They were shiny, these men from the deep, and black in color. They were thorny, too, and armored like a crab. Were they even men? Nikos could not tell, but their actions frightened him further. They had found a body on the beach, and they bent over it, ensuring that it was dead before heading further inland.

The strange patrol moved on, passing directly beneath Nikos' tree and into the town, and Nikos began to climb down the tree and to follow them despite himself. The men were strange and unearthly, yet he couldn't help but wonder where they were headed and why they were there. Once on the ground he followed them at a distance, ducking behind the corners of buildings to examine them while he tried to remain unseen.

As he watched, the visitors seemed to take interest in the damage that the waves had done to the buildings. Inspecting the ruins with the bright light-beams that emanated from their heads, four of them moved from building to building checking for damage while the other two examined the bodies and prodded them occasionally with a spear-like weapon they carried.

As Nikos watched the groups, he leaned against a low wall that had bordered a small garden in front of a house. The wall had been weakened by the waves' pummeling, however, and suddenly and to his horror Nikos found the wall crumbling loudly. It collapsed in front of him, leaving him totally exposed to the invaders. Attracted by the sound they turned as one and shone their head-lights upon him.

Nikos turned and sprinted back the way he'd come, his heart hammering in his chest. Behind him he heard the running feet of the strange men. He had to try to lose them in the maze of Katsopolis' ruined streets. He cut a left at the next corner ahead, still hearing the pounding feet of his pursuers behind him but glad to be out of their lights, even if only temporarily. At the first chance he turned right, then again at the next corner; he was trying his hardest to make a circle, to try to lead them on a wild goose-chase that would throw them off and give him time to hide.

Ahead of him, he saw the remains of a fruit stand that had miraculously survived the deluge of the waves. Onto this he jumped and by climbing up on the top of the canopy's supports he was able to scramble onto the roof of a nearby building. He lay on his stomach, as still as he could be despite his shaking nerves and his pounding heart. Below him, he could see a little of the nearby streets, and he saw the lights as the strange invaders spread out to search for him. He wasn't sure what would happen if they caught him, but he didn't want to find out....

Once satisfied that he could get away with it, Nikos stood up and made his way to a nearby roof near the edge of Katsopolis. Here he crawled to the edge and hung from his fingers before dropping back to the street. After peeking around the corner to make sure none of the marauders were nearby, he took off at a run back toward the beach.

The dunes were soaked and running among them was hard, but he kept going. His goal was to make it to the water line and follow it as far toward the nearby cliffs as he could. He knew of small caves in those cliffs, and he planned to hide there till daylight, or at least until he saw the strangers leave. As he broke from the dunes, however, he stopped in his tracks: out in the water, he could see more of the strange lights approaching Katsopolis. The beams of light struck him, framing him in the stark, harsh glow.

The momentary halt was all his pursuers needed. As he stood there, illuminated briefly in the blazing lights of the newcomers, one of the bizarre men appeared from behind a dune behind him and spread a tough wire-weave net around Nikos. He was unable to run, and he tumbled to the sand.

Like a fish in his father's net, Nikos had been caught.

CHAPTER 4: LONGSHOT TO ADVENTURE

Immediately following his conference with Diana St. Clair, Clifton Storm had sprung into action as he began preparations for the lengthy trip to the Aegean Sea. After Diana left Storm's office, he consulted one of the huge maps on the wall behind his desk. A transatlantic flight would be necessary, and the planned construction of his long-range airship was more than a month away from beginning. His current, longest-range seaplane, a Consolidated Commodore, had just finished its modifications and was ready to go. However, even with the new plane's increased fuel capacity it would never make it all the way to Greece and the Aegean Sea. Recent developments in the world of air-travel—a new mid-ocean "pit stop"—would make this flight a possibility, and Storm began to plan his flight-path: from Miami to New York, then out across the Atlantic to a tiny spot, a place so new that Storm himself had had to note it on the map... beside the spot was written "F.P. 1." From there, he would fly to a rendezvous with his people who were already in that area: a blue-colored thumbtack was stationed near Gibraltar, nearly two-thousand miles away from the F.P. 1. Storm smiled: things were coming together nicely.

Turning to his desk, Storm notified his radio-operations center via his intercom. "This is Storm; I need to send a message to the *Independence*."

The *Independence* was MARDL's seagoing base of operations, a super-ship filled with scientific facilities and constructed for just such a purpose at this. It had been located in the region assisting geologists with the analysis of local minerals, but with something afoul in the region Storm decided to have the craft pull up anchor and meet with them... the mineral-study would just have to wait. He then gave commands to the radio operator for the *Independence* to cease operations temporarily and to travel to the coordinates of a meeting place he calculated they could arrive simultaneously. From there, Storm contacted his armory and equipment-storage depots and requested supplies for the trip. The packing was going to be relatively light, though, as an abundance of equipment would be already available for their use aboard the *Independence.*

After a few further arrangements, Storm left his office with Buddy the terrier in tow. He was stopped at the door by a look from Marie.

"What?" he asked his secretary. Her expression was hard to read, but was a mixture of reproach and whimsy, and maybe even a touch concerned.

"I suppose it's time for me to watch that ugly dog of yours again," she said, "while you go traipsing off to parts-unknown, Mr. Adventurer on the move again and all that?"

Storm chuckled and affected a deep, newsreel-narrator voice. "Yes, it looks like I'm off again to who-knows-where, to face who-knows-what-perils, et cetera. You know that it's part of what I do here, so what's it to you?" Storm leaned against the corner of her desk and crossed his arms. "And Buddy isn't ugly, he's got character." Buddy, meanwhile, had come around to Marie's side of the desk and stood on his hind legs with his paws on her thigh, panting and looking up into her face.

Marie raised an eyebrow at the dog and continued. "I don't want you to get into any trouble out there, Cliff. I... we all want you to come back in one piece." She lowered her head and looked over her glasses at him. "Completely intact."

Storm was a bit bewildered. "Marie, since when have you cared so much about...." He caught her eyes as they almost imperceptibly flicked to Diana as she walked through the room and out the office's front door. "Oh, I get it," Storm smiled teasingly at his secretary. "Don't worry, Marie. I won't let the siren's call lead me to my doom, okay?"

Marie lowered her voice. "She's bad news, Cliff. I know you've heard the phrase 'femme fatale' before, and that's her. You know how she is, always running around on some kind of nutty crusade. She'll get you into all kinds of trouble if you follow her."

Storm quietly told Marie the details of their upcoming flight into the unknown, and her opinion of his upcoming mission alongside Diana softened considerably. Herbert Chalmers had been well-liked by everyone that worked within the MARDL organization, and so Marie was saddened to hear of his disappearance.

"So you see," Storm said as he finished up the mission details, "this isn't one of Diana's usual hunts for lost gold or whatever. This is serious business." Marie nodded thoughtfully, and Storm patted her hand. "I promise," he told her, "I'll come back from this, one hundred percent intact." He winked at her and walked to the door.

"You'd better. You know I'm pretty handy with a sword," she said to him, and Storm raised his eyebrows and nodded before he stepped out of the office and into the glare of the Florida sunshine. He had indeed heard the rumor that she was handy with a blade, and he wasn't sure how much of that was truth. He did know, however, that Diana would find out how skilled Marie was if anything happened to him because of her.

Behind her desk, Marie sighed and looked down. Buddy still gazed up at her, his panting face resembling a wide and comical grin below his mischievous eyes. "What are you looking at?" she said to the dog, and softly patted his head.

Before long, Clifton Storm had rounded up two more of his troubleshooters to accompany him and Diana to the Aegean Sea. The first of these was a wiry older black man with salt-and-pepper hair: this was Storm's chief mechanic, Willy Avis. Storm had met him when he was scouting for a location for the MARDL headquarters in Miami and experienced car trouble. He had taken his coupe to a garage owned by Willy, a veteran of the Great War who had served with the Army's 369th Infantry Regiment (the "Harlem Hellfighters"). The two men immediately struck up a friendship. When learning of the organization that Storm was building, Willy Avis had jumped at the chance to become part of it. Besides being a marvel at repairing anything mechanical, Storm discovered that Willy was also a tough and capable ally to have at his side during the more violent aspects of MARDL's troubleshooting business. This was learned when the two of them took on a local gangster who had been leaning on small businesses like Willy's in the Miami area, and the two men had single-handedly managed to put the gangster's little crime ring on ice.

The second person to join the mission was a mountain of a man: bald and with a drooping mustache and tattoos covering most of his arms, Brock Thurman could have passed for a circus strongman and that's exactly what he had been before joining MARDL as one of Storm's troubleshooters and apprentice-engineers. Despite Brock's size, he maintained a whimsical and childlike glint in his eyes and was perhaps one of the gentler members of the organization... until danger reared its head. At that point, Brock Thurman became a roaring dynamo of action, blazing a swath through the enemy ranks with bullet or fist. Brock was both relieved and annoyed when he learned that another troubleshooting regular—the short, wisecracking pilot, Manny "Skids" Gerard—would not be accompanying them on this mission. Skids was away, having gone back to La Isla de Sangre to help the tiny government there with some aerial mapping of the island's more mysterious valleys. Brock and Skids had a playfully antagonistic friendship, and it was often a source of alternating irritation and entertainment to Storm and the others during their field-work for MARDL.

Once the crew was assembled, the team met at Hangar #2, where the Consolidated Commodore seaplane, fresh from its modifications, was being rolled out for her maiden voyage. The long, thin body was topped with an almost comically-wide 100 ft. wingspan, under which nestled a pair of Pratt & Whitney Hornet radial engines. The craft was painted a deep blue, and painted underneath the raised pilot's cabin was a curvy blonde woman in a tight red body suit. The blonde held a bow and arrow which was drawn and pointed forward toward the plane's nose. Above her, in lighter blue, was the nickname that Storm and his crew had given the Commodore: "*The Longshot.*"

Outside the fence in the distance, the two spies still watched the compound. The sweaty man had returned to his companion after making his phone call earlier in the day: he had been instructed to notify the unseen voice on the other end of the phone if and when Storm and a party had left the compound by airplane. As they watched the Commodore being wheeled down to the water on a dolly, the man with the binoculars muttered to the other one, "Better go make your call again, Fitz, and hurry. We're gonna have to beat it out of here fast if we wanna catch up at the rendezvous."

"I'm goin', I'm goin'..." said the short and sweaty man as he climbed down. "I can't wait to get out of this stinkin' state... it just ain't right, Jimmy. You shouldn't sweat during November!"

"Forget it... they're takin' off. We gotta get to the airfield now, and you can call from there!" said Jimmy as he climbed from the tree.

The duo hastened to their vehicle and piled into it. As their car shot off in the direction of the Pan American airfield to the north, they could see out past the MARDL compound as the *Longshot* lifted gracefully from the water and headed off into the eastern sky. Their quarry was on the move.

...a curvy blonde held a bow and arrow...

CHAPTER 5:
F.P. 1

In the flashes of lightning, the dark ocean seemed to be alive and crawling with waves when seen from the air. Rain, pushed to and fro by the ever-changing wind, was an impenetrable curtain in the night and visibility was low. Eventually, a small spot of light showed itself through the storm, followed soon by searchlights as they blazed out and combed the sky. As the source of the illumination drew nearer more details could be made out from the air... this was no simple ship's light casting its rays out into the gloom.

A broad rectangle of black steelwork supported by massive pontoon floats and topped with a white tarmac platform, Flying Platform #1 was less of an ocean vessel and more than a floating airport. On one broad side of the landing platform was a collection of hangars and cranes as well as a pair of massive elevator platforms that led below the deck to a workshop area. The other side of the platform was dominated by the control tower and adjoining terminals but also featured a host of shops, restaurants, and hotels. Over a quarter-mile in length, F.P. 1 was a fully self-contained and operational waypoint for transatlantic flights to refuel and rest during their arduous and lengthy travel. The storm, however, was lashing at the massive air-station and despite its enormous size it rocked upon the waves of the North Atlantic Ocean.

From out of the southwestern sky, the lights of an approaching plane could be seen through the rain by the control tower, and crews had been dispatched to the #3 crane station as soon as the plane had radioed in and announced its arrival. The seaplane circled low over the island of steel and glass before finally hitting the roiling water. It taxied as best it could to where a crew and a giant harness had been lowered near the rippling surface, and from inside the aircraft a pair of figures scrambled out of the cabin and clambered on top of the wing. It took several minutes for the men to secure the harness to the plane, during which time their electric torches and flashes of lightning illuminated the faces of the plane's crew on the wing: the scarred and lean countenance of Clifton Storm and the bald and mustached visage of Brock Thurman. After the two troubleshooters and the crew from F.P. 1 finally got the crane's harness secured, the men steadied themselves and the signal was given to the winch operator, who slowly and steadily lifted the *Longshot* from the waves. The crane set the plane down upon a wheeled dolly on the deck, and Diana St. Clair & Willy Avis scrambled out of the aircraft to join their comrades on the tarmac. The deck crew secured the Commodore against the lashing wind and rain and wheeled the craft into a waiting hangar. Willy oversaw the securing of the *Longshot*, and then the soaking group made their way toward the terminal structure on the other side of the platform where a waiting figure was outlined in the light of an open door.

"Get in out of the rain, you fools," the figure called. "There's hot coffee and sandwiches waiting for you in here."

"We'd only be fools if we turned down that coffee. We're soaked," said Storm as he shook hands with the man in the doorway. "Long time no see, Droste." He and his crew stepped into the building as Droste shut the door on the raging tempest outside. Storm and the others shrugged out of their dripping raincoats and gratefully accepted towels that Droste handed them from a bin; they then followed him further into the bowels of F.P. 1's terminal to a lounge area, which was warm and comfortable, and he showed them to an urn of coffee and a plate of snacks.

"This is some set-up here," Brock whistled as he gazed about the lounge. The walls were of a rich oak paneling and the floors were thickly carpeted, and beside fully-stocked bookshelves and fine oil-paintings, the room even boasted a fireplace that crackled cheerfully with warmth. The room would not have been out of place in the finest social clubs of New York City, and it was hard to believe that it was in the middle of such a modernistic setting as the F.P. 1.

"Please, sit down," Droste urged the group as he dropped into an overstuffed armchair. He was an intense man with a high forehead, piercing eyes and slicked-back hair. "That storm isn't going anywhere any time soon, so I don't think you'll be rushing off. When I heard you were coming here my curiosity was piqued: the famous mystery man Challenger Storm hasn't been in this area since that business with the industrial espionage that plagued our early days here. I still can't thank you enough for your help."

"Don't thank me yet, the investigation still continues. I doubt we'll ever get to the real people responsible," Storm replied, and then he introduced their host. "Droste, you know Willy and me, of course; this is Diana St. Clair and Brock Thurman. This is Commander B.E. Droste, designer and head honcho of the F.P. 1. The papers and newsreels didn't really reveal the details to the public, but shortly after setting up shop out here the platform was sabotaged by a spy, and that spy's actions very nearly resulted in the deaths of all aboard and the sinking of F.P. 1."

"I took a bullet in the shoulder myself when confronting the spy," Droste interjected. "His name was Damsky and he was my chief engineer, a man I trusted. He had arranged for the full flooding of our ballast tanks and for his escape by motorboat. He got away, but when his boat was found drifting in the Atlantic later, he was discovered dead on board from starvation and exposure. He had perished at sea from a lack of supplies... his masters apparently wanted no loose ends and short-changed his stock of fuel and food and probably just 'failed' to meet him at a rendezvous spot."

"Meanwhile, all of the escape craft on Flying Platform 1 had been crippled by the saboteur and the communications were cut, while a poison gas nearly took all the personnel out," Storm continued. "They'd have been dead and this place would've been history if it hadn't been for Droste's old friend Ellissen and Claire Lennartz..."

"That's Claire *Droste*, now," their host said, smiling. He waggled the ring finger on his left hand where a band of gold shone. "The two of them flew in and pulled us out of the fire with almost no time to spare. Though their plane crashed upon landing, Ellissen managed to fly a Frankenstein's monster of a plane out of here: it was made of spare parts and scrounged gasoline, and it crashed over the ocean. Ellissen was able to parachute into the sea to be picked up by a ship, though, and they radioed for assistance for us. I met Storm some time later while he was aiding the investigation into who had ordered those sabotages on the F.P. 1."

"Sadly, all our leads have become dead ends," Storm said. "I'm still willing to bet it had something to do with shipping tycoons who feel their way of life—or rather their way of wealth—is threatened by transatlantic flight, but there's no evidence for us to use against them... yet."

"Well, your attention to this matter makes all the world of difference, my friend." Droste rose from his chair. "You and your crew are always welcome here. I will attend to your lodgings here at once, and only the finest rooms available will do. Now, if you'll excuse me..." he bade in farewell to his guests and promptly left the room.

As Diana, Willy and Brock moved about the sumptuous lounge Storm leaned back in his chair and closed his eyes, enjoying the restive moment. He had not been planning to stay at F.P. 1 for longer than was necessary, but with the chaotic weather outside he and his team would have to stay until it let up. The surroundings had a calming effect on the group: amazingly, there seemed to be very little movement felt here, and it was almost hard to believe that they were on a massive floating island in the middle of the stormy ocean and not in a luxury skyscraper high above city streets. This could possibly be a last chance to grasp some rest before the troubleshooters journeyed into the unknown, and they had decided to take advantage of this fact and rest.

It was nearly two hours later, after Storm and his troubleshooters had retired to their rooms, that the second plane of the night approached the F.P. 1 from out of the storm. A small passenger model, the Heinkel He 57 was an amphibious plane capable of landing on the ocean as well as on the ground, and once given clearance to land it skimmed in to alight on the tarmac landing platform. Upon landing, the men in this plane made it clear to the deck crew that they would be leaving as soon as they were able to and made arrangements to have their plane made ready to leave again at once, against the better judgment of the air-travel officials onboard F.P. 1.

The three visible passengers of the Heinkel consisted of the same duo who had been the spies outside of the MARDL compound, tall and lanky Jimmy and squat and sweaty Fitz—as well as a third man, a quiet-faced individual with round-rimmed glasses and black curly hair. As Jimmy, Fitz, and their silent partner engaged in conversation with the deck crew, no one noticed a second set of men, a rat-faced individual and a large thug whose general outline seemed to be that of a rectangle, as they snuck out of the Heinkel amphibian plane and stole away into the rain-soaked shadows between the hangars nearby....

Willy Avis hadn't been asleep for long when he woke up suddenly with the strange feeling that something was wrong. Maybe not "wrong," but something nagged at him, tugging at his brain and dragging him from sleep with a sudden surety.

After lying awake for a while in the warmth of his hotel room bed, the aging mechanic muttered to himself, "Ah, to hell with this," and got dressed. He left his room and made his way by elevator to the ground floor of the hotel and terminal complex. He retrieved his raincoat where it had been left to dry by the door and stepped out once again into the night.

The rain was somewhat lighter now, but the wind was no less fierce, and he drew the collar of the raincoat up around his face. Across the expanse of tarmac were the dark hangars: apart from a small crew working at maintaining a small Heinkel the area seemed deserted. Willy looked across toward the hangar that housed the *Longshot* and tried to calm his mind. The MARDL, although not exclusively designed or modified by him alone, were still like his babies, and he cared for each one of the planes as though they were his and his alone. Perhaps it was the weather or the surroundings, or the fact that once again he was accompanying his friend on another journey into adventure… whatever it was, Willy felt the need to check out the *Longshot* once more before sleeping, or he would never get a good night's rest. He started off across the broad platform.

In the *Longhot's* hangar, the rat-faced man and the hulking rectangular tough were busily working by flashlight underneath the MARDL seaplane. They were attaching a device to the fuselage of the aircraft and were having some difficulty in the matter.

"If it was up to me, Oakley," the big thug grunted, "we'd just go up to where they're sleeping and snuff 'em out there. I like getting my hands dirty, but not like this."

"Yeah, well it's not up to you, Packer," the man with the rodent visage declared. "The boss wants this to be as accidental as possible. This little baby is a thing of genius: it activates with the touch of salt-water, so as soon as this bird is lowered into the water the bomb arms itself. After that, the trigger-mechanism is rigged so that fifteen minutes after the bird leaves the water and is far enough away from this dump, the plane goes blooey. No muss, no fuss, and no witnesses… just one less troublemaker and his pals pokin' their nose into our business." He cackled gleefully as he tightened the last of the bomb's fastenings.

"There!" Oakley announced. "It's on and it ain't goin' anywhere. Now let's get out of here and sneak back onto our plane so we can get the hell off this platform. The boss is waiting for word from us, and you know how he gets if we report in late." He and the gorilla-like Packer scrambled up off the floor and hastily began cleaning up the traces of their devious handiwork.

Suddenly the piercing beam of a flashlight framed them against the side of the Commodore. They blinked into the light, momentarily blinded. "Stop right there!" a voice commanded.

Behind the flashlight Willy Avis had the two saboteurs on the spot, but he didn't know for how long he could keep them in line; he had left his pistol in his hotel room and was unarmed, and he'd have to bluff it with two such tough customers such as these. "I don't know who you gentlemen are but that's my plane, and you've got a lot to explain about why you're messing around with it. Now hands up! We're going to see platform security about this."

"Now wait a minute," Oakley protested. "We're mechanics, just doin' a little touchin' up on your plane is all. I got credentials...." He began to reach into his jacket.

"I said freeze!" Willy demanded, stepping closer and hoping his bluff would hold. "It just so happens I'm a mechanic too and I heard part of your conversation. Typically, we try to keep things from going 'blooey' as you put it, not the other way around. We also don't pick the locks of our own hangars or workshops, as you gentlemen so clumsily and obviously did. Now get that hand out of your jacket right now!"

Packer, sure that their discoverer was focused firmly upon Oakley and not paying him any attention, swung a fist out to grab the tall steel cylinder of compressed gas off of a nearby welder's rig. With a speed that was surprising for his size he swung the cylinder through the air and toward Willy.

The mechanic hit the floor, just barely avoiding the hurtling gas cylinder, and he rolled behind a large wheeled tool-chest as Oakley produced his pistol from his jacket. Oakley fired a single shot at the rolling form, just missing him by inches.

Willy cursed himself for forgetting the pistol, and knew there was no way that he could get to the weapons and equipment stored inside the *Longshot*. He got to his feet and turned off his flashlight; he began to move as stealthily as he could through the dark hangar, knowing that now the element of surprise was his only hope.

Oakley and Packer, meanwhile, had shut off their own light and were stalking through the hangar as well, straining their ears for any sound of their quarry. They stepped lightly, waiting to hear the scuff of a shoe or a quick intake of breath through the sound of the drumming rain on the metal roof. They crouched low to help make out any sound of their prey.

Willy Avis crouched above them on a low beam that held equipment. If they had been walking with straight postures they perhaps could have heard the low scrape of Willy's shoes just before he pounced down upon the rat-faced Oakley, who gave a startled scream as the MARDL mechanic swung a heavy wrench down upon the back of his head. The blow was intended to knock him out, but the wrench glanced off something in the dark and it only stunned the thug.

Packer rushed toward the sounds and Willy spun, glimpsing his pouncing form dimly in the light filtering through the hangar windows. He sidestepped Packer like a matador avoiding a bull, and as the thug stumbled by him Willy lashed out with a foot, tripping him. Packer crashed into the tool-chest and it collapsed under his weight, spilling its content of wrenches, screwdrivers, and other tools out onto the concrete floor around him. Willy waited while he heard the big man floundering and struggling to get up. Then like a freight train rocketing from the dark, Packer was on the charge toward him again.

Willy stepped toward him then to the side at the last second, hammering his fist into Packer's solar plexus in a strong, rapid jab. The big man's growl turned into a gasp as he hurtled past his intended target and once again he stumbled as he fell to the hangar floor.

Willy took a chance then: he stabbed a flashlight beam out, first at his opponents as they sprawled on the floor among the scattered tools, then toward the walls of the hangar. He was looking for an alarm switch, something he could use to bring help. Suddenly as he turned toward another wall the faces of lanky Jimmy and sweaty little Fitz were lit up in his beam, and something crashed upon his head before he could strike out at them. A terrible curtain of darkness fell on Willy Avis and he crumpled to the ground.

CHAPTER 6: THE HUNTRESS

"What the hell were you two mugs tryin' to do in here?" Jimmy scolded Packer and Oakley as he brandished the heavy wrench with which he knocked out Willy. "Why didn't you just send a marching band out there? I bet the whole place heard you, you idiots."

"He got the drop on us, Jimmy," rat-faced Oakley protested. "We hadda try and take 'im down quick…"

Jimmy cut him off. "Yeah, well, everybody and their brother's probably gonna be looking into that shot you fired, Oakley. You guys: clean this place up and we'll toss the body overboard, we gotta get the hell out of here pronto!" The four thugs rapidly started straightening the overturned tool-chests and spilled tools. There was a low groan from the floor.

"Holy… hey, this guy's still alive," called Fitz as he bent over the prone figure of Willy Avis. He gave out a yelp as he recognized him. "And this is one of Challenger Storm's guys! We're in deep…"

"Shut up!" big Packer rumbled. "It don't matter who it is, the plan don't change: we dump him over the side like Jimmy said. He's in no condition to swim those waves right now… he'll be fish food before they ever find him." Packer began tying the heavy compressed-gas cylinder to Willy's ankles. "This'll take care of him."

Once they finished cleaning up the mess in the hangar, the four men cautiously left by a rear entrance. Willy was slung limply over Packer's shoulder and Oakley helped to carry the cylinder. The quiet-faced and curly-haired man with glasses stood outside in the driving downpour waiting for the hoods, and he watched them curiously through his round lenses. "Get to the plane and stand nearby," Jimmy commanded him. "Wait for us there, got it?" The man in the glasses nodded slowly and left.

As the four men walked in the opposite direction, Fitz muttered to his comrades: "Geez, but that guy is creepy. I hate when the boss tells us to bring one of those guys along with us."

"We needed him along for the ride, Fitz, to help us get to where we needed to go. Personally, I'll be glad to get away from him, too," Jimmy admitted. Then: "Up ahead here… get that hatch open."

Fitz knelt at the closed portal set flush in the platform's surface. Unlocking it, he raised the round hatch and the men looked down at what was uncovered. Through the round hole, a ladder could dimly be seen: it led downward toward the lower levels of F.P. 1's exterior. Lightning flashed, momentarily illuminating what lay past the ladder and about ten stories straight down: the heaving black surface of the Atlantic Ocean.

"Dump him Packer, he's startin' to wake up," Jimmy ordered. Indeed, Willy was starting to comprehend weakly where he was, though his strength was low. The tank-like goon did as he was told and lifted the mechanic's limp form while Oakley started guiding the heavy cylinder through the hatch….

A shot rang out. It ricocheted off of the hatch-cover next the Fitz's hand, and he whipped it back in sudden fear. The group looked around as they drew pistols… this time there would be no avoiding gunplay.

"Hold it right there!" a voice called. It was a woman's voice that commanded the killers, and they turned toward the sound.

In the distance, Diana St. Clair crouched in the rain on one of F.P. 1's massive aircraft-cranes. In her hands and aimed toward them was her prime weapon of choice: a customized Model 1895 Winchester rifle.

The aviatrix had been unable to sleep when the group had retired to their individual rooms; her mind was in turmoil and on her missing friend and former lover, Herbert Chalmers. She had gone for a walk and was in the vicinity just in time to hear the pistol shot from the hangar. Investigating, she witnessed Willy being carried out of the *Longshot's* hangar by the mysterious group. Never without her rifle, she had climbed up swiftly onto the crane in order to gain the advantage of being able to snipe them… at least she hoped it would work that way.

Diana sighted through its telescopic scope at the group of men and centered her crosshairs on Jimmy's right thigh. "Put him down now!" she called to them. "You won't get another chance."

The thugs hesitated for a moment, then scattered… dropping Willy and the cylinder through the hatch in the process. Diana cursed under her breath as she jumped down from the crane; she scrambled toward the hatch in fear for her friend and ally, praying that he was still all right somehow.

Willy had gained back enough of his consciousness to realize what was happening and miraculously managed to grab the hatch's hinges as he dropped. He was literally hanging by his fingertips now; his body was already weakened from the blow to his head, and he was weighed down further by the gas cylinder tied to his ankles. It swung perilously, threatening to drag him down to the ocean waves below. He gasped air into his lungs helplessly. The hatch was slick with rain, and he felt his fingertips slipping….

Diana threw herself from her sprint into a belly-slide, gripping Willy's wrist as his fingers finally slipped free completely. She had him, but felt his weight pulling her across the wet surface of the platform. She angled her body, bracing it behind the locked-open hatch-cover. She had him, but only momentarily and her grip was clumsy and getting more awkward by the moment. Willy realized that the swinging of the cylinder was harming their struggle, and he managed to swing it gently to where it rested against one of the ladder's rungs, lessening the weight that threatened the two of them. As Diana pulled, he managed to use his other arm to grab another rung of the ladder. So long as he made sure the gas cylinder was wedged against the rung below him, he wouldn't have to worry about being pulled from his perch on the ladder.

"I'm okay, Diana, I got the ladder now. Go on, stop those guys from getting away," he told her. She nodded and after making sure that both his hands and feet were on the ladder she let go of his arm. She took off in the direction of her quarry.

Ahead of the fleeing group, an F.P. 1 security officer stepped from around the corner of one of the workshops, alerted by the sound of gunshots. "Hey!" he called toward the running group as he swung his flashlight's beam up and into their eyes. The security man was met with several shots from their pistols, and he ducked back around the corner. He slid back the bolt on his submachine gun and got ready to confront them, but a massive hand suddenly swung around the corner and wrapped itself around his neck. The security officer felt himself being lifted from his feet and his Thompson was plucked from his loosening fingers. Packer swung the officer and his victim seemed to fly from his fist. Grinning, the bloodthirsty thug snatched up the gun and sighted along its barrel at its former owner. He began to squeeze the trigger as his comrades rushed toward the Heinkel in the distance.

Once again a single shot rang out, but this time it drew blood from Packer's arm. Packer's arm dropped limply and the gun clattered to the ground. He spun angrily and witnessed Diana at the rear of the alleyway, her Winchester aimed for his heart. She fired, and her shot would have sped true if it weren't for Jimmy, the group's de facto leader, as he yanked Packer away from the mouth of the alley between hangars. Diana's bullet ripped through empty air, and she sprinted up from her crouch and ran toward the other end of the alley. She couldn't let the group get away. She had to stop them.

By now, all of F.P. 1 had broken out into bedlam: the sound of a high-pitched siren split the air. From the towers searchlights were springing into life and their beams swept across the tarmac. From loudspeakers a voice was shouting at the fleeing thugs with orders to halt, while the platform's meager security forces had taken up positions and were preparing to shoot the men down if they did not comply.

The thugs' answer was simple: Oakley and Fitz began firing indiscriminately toward the security men. F.P. 1's civilian patrons, roused from their sleep by the activity, had been trickling out onto the terminal's balconies; they now scattered at the sound of the gunshots and a woman began to scream in hysterics. The platform's security men returned fire.

"This'll shut 'em up," growled Jimmy as he reached beneath his coat. He pulled forth a grenade and yanked the pin, lobbing it toward the nearest cluster of blue-uniformed security men. They tried to scatter as the pineapple-shaped explosive bounced among them but there was no room: they had chosen several tightly-grouped pieces of equipment to use as cover. Their scramble was in vain.

Clifton Storm vaulted over the balcony railing above them. He landed nearly on top of the grenade, and he hastily grabbed it up and hurled it across the tarmac toward an unoccupied hangar. The grenade never made it. Its timer expired, the grenade went off in mid-air and rained debris and shrapnel everywhere with a thunderous roar.

Storm was already in action, climbing over the equipment and throwing himself forward into a sprint toward the Heinkel plane. Behind him big Brock Thurman had reached the platform and was following as best as he could. Ahead of Storm in the distance the attackers had nearly reached the plane and the strangely quiet and curly-haired man waited for them there.

As he passed by a drum of fuel outside one of the workshops, Packer stopped and yanked the barrel's stopper free with his good hand, then kicked the drum over. The liquid splashed and spread out in a widening puddle between him and their pursuers. Packer grinned and brought out a cigarette lighter; he flicked it into action and tossed the flaming device into the puddle. With a whoosh, the puddle leaped into a conflagration, lighting the center of F.P. 1's tarmac into a flaming orange wall.

Oakley's rat face split open into a vicious cackle. "Good one, meat-head," he congratulated his ally. "Let's see 'em get by that!"

Storm, Brock and Diana reached the wall of fire together and they raised their weapons to fire upon the group as they were piling into the Heinkel. The craft's engine was already turning over and if the troubleshooters didn't try to stop the group they might never get to the bottom of what was happening.

Diana peered through the scope at the group and suddenly gasped in astonishment at the sight of the curly-haired man with the glasses with the thugs. She dropped her rifle. "Don't shoot!" she cried, throwing Storm's aim up. "You could hit him!"

"What? Hit who?"

"Herbert!"

Chalmers! Storm looked back to the Heinkel. Somehow, not only was Herbert Chalmers here but he was with this group for some reason. It didn't make sense, but they had to get answers before it was too late.

Storm spun and ran in the opposite direction for several feet before he stopped and reversed directions. With a running start he now ran straight toward the fiery barrier. At the last second, he leaped. His powerful jump didn't clear the fire completely, but it did carry him through to the other side. He hit the ground at the edge of the flame-wall, his right pant-leg and shirt-sleeve on fire. He rolled over and over, stifling the flames on his clothing before springing back to his feet when the flames were out. He broke into a run again for the escaping Heinkel and its passengers in the distance.

The aircraft was rolling now and was gaining speed as it neared the edge of the runway. Storm ran as though it was all he had ever known, his entire world narrowed to the single goal of catching up with the Heinkel and stopping them before it was too late. The plane was going to have a short take-off, he thought. They *had* to stop or they would risk plunging into the Atlantic.

The plane reached the end of the platform and it dropped from sight. Storm reached the edge just as the plane disappeared and he suddenly found himself teetering there on the brink above the drop to the waves below. His arms pinwheeled as he fought for balance, and even as he floundered there helplessly he saw the Heinkel struggle, then right itself. It narrowly leveled out over the water and climbed up into the night sky, its engine roaring in a mocking triumph.

His balance regained, Storm stepped back from the edge of the platform and watched as the craft sped away into the darkness of the turbulent ocean night. He felt helpless, and he shouted though his clenched teeth in frustration.

CHAPTER 7: RENDEZVOUS WEST OF GIBRALTAR

After the escape from the Platform, Commander Droste immediately attempted to scramble one of F.P. 1's pursuit planes after the fleeing saboteurs. They were unable to give chase: crews discovered that the pursuit-aircraft had been disabled by the thugs as well, covering their tracks in the possibility that they would have been found out and followed before their work had been completed. For the time being, the mysterious attackers would have to remain an enigma.

Accepting their temporary defeat, Storm and Brock helped F.P. 1's fire-crew to put out the fuel-blaze while Diana St. Clair raced back to check on Willy Avis. The aging mechanic had an egg-sized lump on the back of his head where he had been struck by the goons, but otherwise he was uninjured and he quickly related the events in the hangar as he knew them to Diana. As a precaution Willy was then taken to F.P. 1's small yet fully-functional hospital for a full examination. After seeing him off, Diana caught up with her comrades once the flames had been put out. After she related all the details of the incident the trio went with Commander Droste to the hangar where the *Longshot* was housed.

The bomb on the MARDL plane was soon discovered, and after carefully removing and defusing the device, Storm was able to determine that the triggering mechanism would have allowed them to get airborne and on their way for a considerable distance before blowing up and sending their craft into the ocean's embrace. Brock took the bomb to dispose of it while Diana stayed with Storm as he finished repairing the *Longshot*. Left alone in the hangar, the two were silent for a long time.

"Well," Storm finally said as he sat down on a stool in the hangar and wiped the streaked grease from his face, "someone knew that we were coming, and they didn't want us to get any closer." He paused and fixed his blue-grey eyes on Diana's. "Herbert…" he began after a moment.

"I don't know what he was doing with them, Cliff," she replied quietly.

"I don't know what he was doing with them, Cliff."

"He'd never put my life—*our* lives—in any danger. You know that."

"I do, Diana… or I did. Something could have made him turn on us, though. I hate to say it, but so many people have a price. Promises of money or power… maybe whoever those guys are have some kind of leverage over him. Is there anything they could use to blackmail him with?" His eyes searched hers, finding their gaze steady but carrying a tinge of hurt.

"Cliff… you *know* he wouldn't sell any of us out. Herb's as square as they come. He'd rather die before he'd…"

Storm waved his hand dismissively and stood up. "I know, Diana. It just doesn't make sense. You said they didn't seem to be threatening him, and that he was just following along as they got into their plane. I can't see him just willingly going along with those guys. And he would never have told them where you would go in this kind of situation…." He looked up from his dirty overalls to find her crystal-blue eyes on his and something inside him melted. Storm was suddenly very aware of how close they were, of how badly he had once wanted her in his life outside of their working relationship.

"She's bad news, Cliff," Marie had said to him before they'd left Miami. Her words now echoed in his head….

"Uh, boss?" A rapping on the open door jolted Storm out of the moment, and he and Diana looked toward Brock framed against the light from the rising sun. He jerked his head back toward the terminal. "A radio transmission just came in from Captain Horne. He says the *Independence* is at the meeting coordinates and they've dropped anchor to wait for us."

"Thanks, Brock. We'd better get ourselves in gear." Then to Diana: "After you." She led the way out of the hangar with Storm following.

As Storm passed Brock at the door the bald strongman raised an eyebrow impishly.

"What?" Storm asked.

Brock simply put his hands up in silent acquiescence and grinned as he followed his friend and leader across the tarmac.

Willy Avis recovered quickly from the blow to his head and was ready for action, despite the protests from F.P. 1's chief medical officer. The salty mechanic insisted on being present as the *Longshot* was prepared for flight and he made sure to watch anyone who came near the Commodore with suspicion.

Soon, with the morning sun glistening off of the blue waters of the North Atlantic, the wide-winged seaplane was lowered into the waves by one of F.P. 1's cranes. It taxied out into open water before lifting majestically from the surface with Storm at the controls. The waving personnel on the platform bid the craft goodbye and soon it was lost in the sky, a receding dot in the East.

It flew into the rising sun, miles of deep blue passing below them. Several times they passed over shipping or fishing vessels, but none showed any signs of distress. At one point, Diana spotted a school of dolphins as they leaped and played in the water, and Storm dropped the *Longshot*'s altitude as they passed over the playful mammals. It was an idyllic day to be making the flight, and it was almost easy for the crew of troubleshooters to forget their mysterious mission and the attempt that had been made on their life.

Soon they neared the coast of Portugal and Morocco and there, several miles west of the Straits of Gibraltar, they saw the *Independence* anchored at the rendezvous point.

The MARDL super-ship was a fortress on the water, resembling nothing less than the marriage between cargo freighter and cruise ship. Well over a thousand feet long and over two hundred feet high, the *Independence* was festooned with edifices: workshops, laboratories, and operations centers. It was an impressive and imposing craft, with a black hull sporting a wide aqua-green band below its pristine white deck structures.

After radioing the control-center of their arrival, Storm circled the *Longshot* around the massive craft to give Diana and Brock, who had never seen the *Independence* before, an ample view of the ship. After gently setting the modified Commodore down onto the waves, he taxied the craft toward the starboard side of the giant boat. Suddenly, the side of the *Independence* split open as massive doors rolled back to the sound of a warning klaxon.

The space revealed inside by the opening doors was a fully functional, if compact, seaplane hangar inside the ship's lowest section. Planes and small boats could be launched from this space during calm seas. Bathed in the glare of powerful lights, the *Longshot* glided to a halt and gently bumped into the rubber-protected lower-deck of the launch bay. Uniformed crewmen swarmed the craft to secure it as the waterproof outer doors slid shut, and after Storm and company climbed out the craft was once again lifted by crane. It was brought to a servicing station in the hangar's upper level as powerful pumps drained the seawater from the bay's pool below. Diana and Brock noted that besides several seaplanes hanging from cranes and supports there was also a number of smaller boats that could be launched from the bay with a minimum of preparation; hanging among these was a sort of small submarine craft, though this was in the far reaches of the cavernous hangar-like space and was drenched in shadow. Storm and Willy greeted the head of surface-level launch operations, who was a jovial and barrel-chested roughneck named Gibb, and after exchanging pleasantries and introductions Storm led the others to a nearby elevator which rocketed them up to the upper-levels of the *Independence*.

In the elevator, Diana turned to Storm. "Cliff… I'd heard about this ship before, but I had no idea it would be so big, and that so many people would be staffing it. Exactly how many people do you have on the MARDL payroll?"

Storm looked into space blankly, then cocked his head and frowned. Finally, he shook his head and grinned. "I don't really know," he said sheepishly. "Marie keeps track of all the nuts and bolts, paychecks and personnel…. Thank God for her, or I'd be lost."

Willy and Brock exchanged a quick smile; as much as Storm was renowned as a globe-trotting adventurer, designer, and creator of the sprawling and many-armed MARDL organization, he was also clueless when it came to the work of organizing and running its regular business. His eternally exasperated secretary was every bit the medium through which MARDL ran smoothly, and the fact quietly embarrassed Storm: he had vowed to better himself in every way, to become a man of science and adventure and a force for good in the world and yet could barely organize his own operations.

After exiting the elevator, the group made their way to the ship's deck to find the Captain of the *Independence*, Peter Horne, waiting for them.

A rangy and rough-looking middle-aged man from Manchester, England, Horne greeted them warmly. He too was familiar with Storm and Willy Avis, but had never met Brock or Diana, whose hand he kissed in as chivalrous a manner as he could with a devilish smile. After introductions, he turned to Storm.

"Thought you should know about this, sir," he addressed Storm as he handed him a sheet of typewritten information. "This morning, the fishing village of Katsopolis was found completely wiped out. Buildings knocked around, bodies everywhere, people missing…. The authorities think a tidal wave hit it."

"A tidal wave?" Storm queried. "There's been no recent history of tidal wave-activity in that area... maybe they're due for one. No survivors, though?"

"None that have been found yet."

"Damn... have your men keep an ear on it, Captain. If we can help them in any way, we will."

"Aye, sir. In the meantime, we're all set: refueled in Spain and ready to sail. Shall we...?" He jerked his head to the east.

Storm nodded. "Let's go, Captain."

Captain Horne gave the orders to the engine room, and soon the gigantic and powerful ship was cutting through the waves with a surprising speed for such a large craft; the amazingly strong and efficient engines were a testament to the MARDL engineers' skill. The *Independence* was soon speeding its way past Spain and Morocco and heading toward the Aegean Sea.

CHAPTER 8: POSEIDON

While the *Independence* sped its way toward the investigation, the four thugs who had failed to sabotage the *Longshot* at Flying Platform 1 were suddenly in a curious position: they were suddenly feeling envious of the fifth member of their group. Herbert Chalmers, the strangely robotic "advisor" that had accompanied the group on their mission, had no need to report to their superior and so was sent to his quarters when they returned to their hidden base of operations. Fitz, Jimmy, Packer, and Oakley watched Chalmers as he disappeared into the labyrinthine tunnels of the dank and dimly-lit cave. They hesitated, stalling for as long as they could before Jimmy finally muttered, "Okay, might as well get this over with."

The four men headed down a separate tunnel, one that went high up a gentle incline. After a turn, the tunnel wall opened up and their path became a metal catwalk spanning the ceiling of a massive cave. On their right, the opening afforded them a view of the huge grotto below. Their boat was moored to a dock there, and the reflections of floodlights anchored to the cave's ceiling bounced off the water and created ever-shifting shapes on the walls. To their left they were given an ample view of the deeper reaches of the enormous space and the things that waited there…. It was an amazing sight to see, but the men surely didn't feel like admiring the view. They begrudgingly marched onward.

The catwalk ended in another tunnel on the opposite side of the grotto and their course began winding its way into the walls of the cave again, twisting and turning and branching off in other directions. Sometimes in the lights affixed to the cave walls they would pass one of their comrades, and other times another numb-acting minion like Herbert Chalmers. They followed their course from memory, winding their way finally to where the tunnel widened. Here, rough-hewn steps were carved in the stone floor that led upward to a concrete wall set with a heavy metal door; this door was flanked by a pair of rough-looking customers, each armed with a submachine gun.

They approached the door and Jimmy, who had been the leader of the mission, muttered a password to the guards. A member of the stone-faced duo nodded silently before knocking on the door. From inside, an imperious voice boomed a reply: "Enter." With a metallic thud, the door unlocked itself using a hidden mechanism and it swung open.

The cavernous space revealed inside was the inner sanctum of the man who called himself Poseidon. The dome-like room had a high ceiling, the top of which was set with a cleverly disguised circular skylight, and this allowed sunlight to stream down into the room in a single pillar of light. The dimmer corners of the room were lit with torches, though several electric lamps burned over a series of desks and tables in the rear of the space. The furniture of the room was Grecian in design, and through an arched doorway in the rock another room could be glimpsed holding a mammoth bed. The center of the main room, however, was dominated by an ancient golden throne: this had been plucked from the sea and carefully and lovingly restored to its former glory by Poseidon himself. Beside the throne was a simple table holding a pair of items: a long and flowing toga that had been carefully draped across the table's surface, and a delicately-wrought plaster mask. This depicted the Greek god from whom Poseidon had taken his name and resembled a fearsome bearded man, glowering and framed by a lion-like mane of hair.

Upon the throne was Poseidon.

Clad in a black turtleneck sweater and black trousers, he regarded the visitors with dark eyes beneath lowered eyelids. His hair had been allowed to grow long, and it was streaked here and there with grey, as was the heavy mustache that covered his lip. His jaw was firm and his chin dimpled, and his cheekbones stood out from his lean and heavily-tanned face. He was a man who obviously had spent many years in the sun and out at sea. He looked nearly asleep, and he slumped sideways in his regal chair. His chin rested in his right hand as he regarded the four men, and his left hand held a crystal goblet of sherry.

Behind them, the door to Poseidon's lair clanged shut, and they suppressed the urge to jump at the sound.

"Jimmy, Oakley, Packer, Fitz: you bring me good news, I hope...?" His voice was low in the cavernous space.

"We, uh... we don't think we got them, boss." Fitz spoke up after the others were quiet for several moments.

There was silence.

"What Fitz means is we didn't see the plane blow up, but we didn't see them get the bomb off of it either, boss," Jimmy stated, attempting to provide a damage-controlling spin to the events aboard F.P. 1. "We'd just finished installing the bomb on Storm's crate but we got stopped by one of his men. He was a scrapper, but we got the better of him. We tried to dump him over the side but we got caught. There was plenty of bullets flying around… Packer got winged." At this the brutish Packer brought up his bandaged arm in its sling for Poseidon to see. "We stalled 'em with one hell of a fire, then we got out of there." Jimmy laughed weakly. "They're probably still tryin' to put those flames out…"

"I didn't ask you to start a fire," Poseidon interrupted. "I asked you to *kill Storm and his crew!*" This last exclamation rose from the quiet tones that he had used before to a thunderous roar that echoed off the domed ceiling of the cave, and he flung the goblet of sherry at the thugs. It struck the wall behind them and showered them with glass.

Poseidon rose to his feet… he was tall, nearly seven feet in height, and he towered over the men. "I *knew* that girl had been poking around, I *knew* she would be going to Storm for help. Since we were too late to stop her, I knew we could catch up with them at F.P. 1 and that this was our chance to get them out of our hair before they became a problem. What I *didn't know* was that I'd be sending a bunch of apes out to do my bidding. I don't hire apes, I hire professionals!"

Poseidon had been pacing before his throne as he ranted. He now turned his attention to his four minions and was coming down the steps, slowly advancing upon his men.

"Jimmy," he said. "I expected you to be a leader, to be my guiding hand when I could not be there. You failed me. You know that I have ways of making you more obedient…"

"Aw, no, boss!" Jimmy protested. "Look, gimme another chance, please. I can do it. We can stop him… I got ideas, see!"

Poseidon was silent for a moment, his face shadowed. The only sound in the chamber was the crackling of the torches and the faint hum of electricity. "You have your second chance, Jimmy," he said slowly. "Fail me again and you join Chalmers and the others. Now go, all of you." At this the four thugs hurriedly left the room, the heavy door rapidly slamming shut behind them.

Left alone once again, Poseidon mounted the steps and walked to the middle of the dome-shaped throne-room. Here, he stared upward in contemplation through the round skylight in the ceiling and at the clear blue sky high above.

CHAPTER 9: MYSTERIES FROM THE DEEP

Sometime later, on the private yacht Fair Game, *somewhere in the eastern region of the Aegean sea...*

"I can't stay out in the sun too long, I have a tendency to freckle," the short, stocky and bespectacled man whined. "Geez, my stomach's all torn up... why did I come out here?"

"Because it was a free trip to Greece, and you have no job and nothing better to do right now," his tall and horse-faced friend replied and grinned wryly. He had the easygoing manner of a nightclub entertainer which is, in fact, what he was. "What else would you be doing right now?"

"...I'd be doing stuff," the other man assured him, taking a sip of his Bromo-Seltzer. He didn't sound too convincing.

"I guess you probably wouldn't be throwing your lunch up into the sea, so there's a feather·in your cap," quipped a feminine voice behind them. They turned as a small woman, her cloud of curly dark hair tucked under a broad-brimmed sun-hat, came up to the yacht's deck from below. She leaned on the railing. "Havin' a good time, boys?"

"Don't listen to the whiner over there," the horse-faced man replied. "It really feels good to get away from New York for a while. I'm really gonna have to thank your father for letting us all use his yacht; this is some ship."

"Uh-uh, no way.... Let her do it," the bald and stocky man said. "He's too scary."

The girl rolled her eyes and started to say something in response but she was interrupted.

"Hey, guys!" a voice called up from the water below. "You should see this water, it's beautiful!" The trio on the deck leaned over the railing to spot their friend, a lanky bird-like individual with a stiff crest of wavy hair. He was swimming in the blue-green waters below.

"Yeah, we're in the middle of the sea, numbskull," the thin man called down sarcastically. "We're surrounded by water. I'm pretty sure we know what it looks like by now." He rolled his eyes.

"Nah, ya gotta see it up close, like the fish do!" the swimming man called up insistently. "That's the only way to see it."

"Hey, be careful," the balding worrier called to his friend. "You don't know what could be down there with you."

"Ah, you worry too much," the swimmer scoffed, "there's nothing more natural." He began swimming again.

The woman called back down to him: "Yeah, well, you know what else is natural? Sharks. Sharks are natural. Man-eating octopuses are natural." She turned to her friend in the glasses who was squinting at her quizzically.

"'Man eating octopuses?'" he asked incredulously.

She shrugged, her face sheepish. "Well… it could happen."

"Hey, what's that over there?" the entertainer said, squinting into the sun and pointing. "That looks like… ice? What is that, ice and some rags on top or something?"

"Where?" the swimming companion asked, floundering in the water. Then he saw it floating about thirty or forty feet away. "I'm gonna go look," he called back up before setting out toward the mysterious object.

He neared his destination and became more puzzled. It did, indeed, look like a misty white-colored block of ice floating in the warm waters of the Aegean Sea. But how was such a thing possible? By all conventional reasoning, it should be melted out there in the heat and warm surface-water.

Reaching the ice, he grabbed a hold of it and found that although it felt cool and smooth, it didn't really feel like ice at all: it didn't have the cold-burn of ice upon his skin. He pulled himself up and onto the irregular block, which was about four feet across. He turned to look at his friends on the yacht not far away before he turned his attention to the pile of clothes that was clinging to the strange ice. After examining it for a moment he saw something strange about the shape.

"What the…?" He bent and gently turned the shape over.

"What is it?" the entertainer called from the yacht.

The "bundle of rags" turned out to be a corpse: it's bloated, decomposing face revealed itself as the bird-like swimmer turned it over. The swimmer straightened, his eyes bulging and his body convulsing suddenly in fear and disgust.

"Oh… oh, mama!" he screamed hoarsely before his feet slipped off the strange ice block and he fell back into the water.

The crew of the *Fair Game* assisted in pulling the strange ice block and its dead passenger aboard, and then a notification of their find was radioed out. It was answered, almost immediately, by the vigilant radio operator aboard the *Independence*. The reply requested that the yacht drop anchor and hang on to the strange findings until they could arrive. The super-ship then set a course for the yacht's location and Captain Horne ordered the engines red-lined.

It was another six and a half hours before the *Independence* entered the Aegean and arrived at the yacht and its awed crew and passengers. A launch motored from the MARDL ship to the *Fair Game*, and it carried Clifton Storm along with its crew and the MARDL doctor, Donald Foster, who had recently been assigned to the *Independence*.

The tourists had been squeamish but the crew of the luxury vessel had managed to get the body and the strange mini-iceberg below deck and into one of the bedrooms. "There's no way I'm sleeping in there now!" Storm heard the whining and stocky man say to one of his friends, and he smiled. The adventurer briefly interviewed the crew and tourists for details regarding the find, then went below deck where Doc Foster was giving the corpse a cursory inspection. He and some of the other MARDL crew bundled the body together along with the weird ice—which was surprisingly light and didn't seem to be melting at all—and carried them from the ship. Before he left, Storm advised the quartet of New Yorkers and their crew to get out of the Aegean as soon as possible and of the possible and unknown danger facing vessels in the area. Bidding them goodbye, he boarded the launch and made way for the return trip to the *Independence*.

Upon their arrival back on their ship, Storm left Doc Foster in charge of the autopsy of the corpse while he had the ice-block sent to one of the ship's labs. Donning green-and-black lab-clothing and covering his face with a protective filter mask and goggles, Storm and an assistant began examining the bizarre find...

Two hours later, a weary Clifton Storm stood outside the laboratory with a cup of coffee in his hand. He wiped the sweat from his brow and massaged his cramped neck-muscles; the investigation had been grueling and had required extensive work to pick the puzzle apart. The "ice" had turned out not to be ice at all and instead had revealed itself to be some kind of plastic-like epoxy. The base temperature of the block had indeed somehow been significantly lower than that of its surroundings, and this gave it the cool feeling when touched. The cause of the bizarre temperature effect was revealed to Storm and the ship's scientists as a byproduct of whatever chemical compound that made the stuff, but the purpose and origin of the substance still eluded the adventurer. Besides the mystery of the "ice" substance itself, there were a few others: on one side the block looked as though it had broken free from a larger piece of the substance, and then there were some odd scoring and scratch-marks on the other side near the dried blood from the body....

The lab's intercom buzzed, and Storm thumbed the receiver. The voice that greeted him was Doc Foster's. "Well, it's over and done with... and I've found some odd things."

"Why doesn't that surprise me?" Storm asked, glancing through the glass window at the strange "ice" in the lab beyond. "Gimme a few minutes, Doc, I'll be right down."

Shortly afterwards, Clifton Storm, still garbed in his laboratory outfit, stepped off the ship's elevator and into a sterilized white hallway. He passed numerous doorways until he came to a pair of heavy metal double-doors marked "MED. BAY-C." He entered them.

The ship's small morgue was dark, save for the white light over the examining table and a yellow-shaded lamp on the desk beyond it. At this desk, Doc Foster looked up as Storm entered. He was an athletic man with jet black hair and a pair of black rimmed glasses who looked more like a football player than a medical doctor. He rose from his desk as Storm made his way through the room and toward the examining table. "Hey, boss... welcome to the freak-show."

Storm looked down at the sheet-covered body on the steel table before him. "That doesn't sound good, Doc. What'd you find?"

"Well, the subject was aged twenty. He had identification on him: his name's Robert Culver. He was an American and I've already sent someone to wire back to the states to get some more information about him. He'd been dead for anywhere between four and ten days. I think he may have been wounded and managed to climb out of the water and onto the block he was found on before he died."

Storm nodded. "I'm with you there. There were some little marks, like fingernail scratches, on one side of the stuff."

Doc Foster nodded gravely and showed Storm scrapings from under Culver's nails: the milky-white substance of the strange "ice." Storm then told Foster about the substance and his findings. "Curiouser and curiouser..." the doctor said, quoting from "Alice's Adventures in Wonderland." He stood thoughtfully for a moment before continuing.

"Okay, now, the cause of death seems to be a pretty obvious thing in this case," Foster said as he donned a pair of surgical gloves and approached the body. He pulled the sheet back to expose Culver's corpse, and the decomposing remains of the scrappy young sailor met Storm's eye once again. "This poor guy had holes punched through his vital organs, three of which went right through his body and out through exit wounds in the back... obviously, that will kill anybody if the holes are in the right spot. It was when I started looking into the fourth hole—the one that didn't go all the way through—for a lodged bullet that I really started scratching my head."

He wheeled a large microscope over to the ragged hole and after focusing it into the wound he invited Storm to look through it. After several moments of examination, Storm pulled himself away. "Well, I don't see a bullet, Doc. But I'm no expert here, you are. What are you seeing?"

Foster nodded. "No, you got it right: there's no bullet. There's no evidence of it being removed, and of course it wouldn't have just fallen out. The tunnels of all of his wounds are ragged, unfocused if you will," he said as he moved the microscope away from the body. "I thought that maybe the projectiles used were some kind of archaic bullets, like rifle balls or something like that. But then I started seeing them on a microscopic level in all of the wounds: hundreds of tiny scratches and abrasions on the tissue in the wound. And lodged in them: crystallized sea salt."

"Well, he *was* found in salt water..." Storm began, unsure of what Foster was describing exactly. The doctor shook his head.

"You don't understand what I'm saying, Cliff. This man was killed *with* salt water. The salt in it must have been compressed into slightly larger crystals than normal, which would account for the salt not completely dissolving in his blood... but the final conclusion is that someone or something punched holes into him with simple water."

Storm's demeanor darkened and the intensity that seemed to emanate from his body seemed to grow stronger. Something stranger had just been brought into this affair, and the weirdness tantalized him.

"That's not possible," he said finally. "The pressure needed to do such a thing would be enormous."

"I know." Foster nodded, covering up Culver and returning to his desk. He picked up a sheet of paper with some notes scribbled on it. "I did some research and found that it would take 461.7 pounds per square inch to break human skin, but at 1500 to 3000 PSI, water would tear into the skin and do serious internal injury... like that." He looked up at Storm.

"Something's out there that's able to do this to flesh and bone."

The men were silent, deep in thought for a long moment. The intercom buzzer shattered the stillness. The doctor pressed the button. "Foster," he said.

The voice that returned from the intercom speaker was the doctor's lab-assistant. "Doc, we just got word back from the states about the DOA. Robert Culver was a sailor on board the cargo steamer *Arapaho*. He's from one of the missing ships."

CHAPTER 10:
S.O.S.

t was nearing midnight. Along with a small lab and workshop, Clifton Storm's cabin had a small adjoining office, and he sat there now pondering the strange events that had brought him and his crew to the Aegean mystery. Before him were information files he'd gathered from his home base in Florida, details regarding each ship and their known passengers, reports on the political climate in Greece, weather reports....

He rested his head in his hands, deep in thought. Unsure of where to look next, he began to look for a connection, something that all the ships or their crew had in common. So far, there were no links, nothing to tie the events together. He looked out his office window, out across the dark expanse of nighttime sea. "What the hell's going on out there...?" he mused to himself quietly.

Returning to his files, he went back to the beginning. The first ship to disappear, a research-vessel called the *Dryad*, belonged to the explorer and oceanographer Roderick Manton. He had been in the area with a team of scientists investigating underwater seismic phenomena and sub-aquatic volcanic activity. His crew and staff of scientists, including the ex-MARDL member Herbert Chalmers, were all tops in their field and like Manton they were all men of high-repute. The last known location of the *Dryad* was somewhere west of the Cyclades. One day the crew from the ship made a deep dive to study sediment on the seabed. The next morning they missed a radio check-in and that was it... they were gone completely from the face of the Earth.

The second ship disappeared about two months later. This ship was the *Blue Princess*, which was an ironically beautiful name for such a utilitarian ship: it had been hauling material and crews for a construction job at Crete. It was owned by Reagan Metalworks, and Steven Reagan, the company's founder himself, had been on board. Storm's brow creased as he looked for more information on the *Blue Princess*... there wasn't anything at all among the files in regards to what they would be building once they arrived. "Purpose: construction" was about the only specifics he could find. Why wasn't that information available in public records?

He searched through the paperwork on his desk for more information about the *Blue Princess'* mission, and this caused several of the files to spill off the edge of his desk and onto the floor. In exasperation, he looked around the office: it had been completely clutter-free upon his arrival on the *Independence* and in his relatively short time onboard he had managed to somehow mess it up enough to mirror his office back home at the MARDL compound. He smiled as he recalled his vivacious and ever-patient secretary, Marie, and her constant efforts to keep things clean around the office… she was so often a perfect yin to his yang.

He got up and went around to the other side of the desk to retrieve the spilled files when his eyes settled on something on one of Roderick Manton's fact-sheets. Business partnerships and known affiliations were listed on this sheet and among these typed lines Storm's eyes zeroed in on one particular name: Steven Reagan.

Storm returned to his seat with the retrieved files and began reading anew, absently taking a sip of cold coffee and making a pinched face as he swallowed. Manton had been a business partner with Reagan several times in the past before their disappearances. Beside his business associations, Manton was a social friend of the industry-man, who was well known both for the innovative constructions that his company built and for his long history of providing rehabilitated criminals with job opportunities. In fact, the construction crew aboard Reagan's ship had been made up of ex-cons bound for the construction project. Through his own philanthropic work, Storm had met Reagan before a few times himself and he admired the man's sense of charity. Was this a coincidence that Reagan just happened to disappear in the Aegean just a short time after his friend, Roderick Manton? And why was there so little information on what Reagan and his ship were heading toward when they disappeared?

He made some notes on a nearby pad and set it aside, then continued to peruse the files that pertained to the eight other ships that disappeared. These soon proved to be just random cargo or large passenger crafts, and nothing tied them to either Reagan Metalworks or Roderick Manton and his scientific team. These were most likely not connected to whatever was behind the mystery… but exactly what was behind it? Storm, though a skeptic, was not above considering the other-worldly aspects of the situation… the supposed "curse" that was claiming ships. And now what of the freak tidal wave that wiped out Katsopolis? Was that even tied together with the other mysteries at all?

Something strange was indeed going on in the Aegean Sea, but before Storm could think of a supernatural cause, he would have to consider a logical, man-made force behind "Poseidon's curse"....

It was now well past midnight. Most of the crew of the *Independence* had settled into bed, leaving the ship's nighttime skeleton-crew to their posts. The after-hours radio man, Horton, sat at his post with earphones clamped to his head. He repeatedly tossed a baseball into the air with his right hand and caught it with the catcher's mitt on his left, all the while staring at the ceiling. The night was, as usual, dull and uneventful. The only sound in his headphones was the soft static of the quiet sea as his advanced radio-set automatically scanned through the frequencies.

Suddenly a noise blasted through the static: a staccato burst of rapidly-tapped Morse code beeps, beginning with the repeated pattern "... --- ...": "S.O.S." Hurriedly, Horton ripped off his catcher's mitt and left the baseball bouncing forgotten on the floor, and he began to jot down the distress message pouring through the aether....

Sometime later, the massive doors on the *Independence* rolled open to reveal the ship's flooded and ready docking-bay. A floatplane was the first to emerge from inside the huge vessel: the aircraft was a small and fast two-person plane armed with a machinegun turret.

After taxiing out into open-water, it picked up speed before lifting off from the water and heading into the west. From the cockpit of the craft, a yellow scarf fluttered in the wind; the helmeted and goggled visage of Diana St. Clair watched the dark waves below as she headed off toward the rough coordinates provided by the frantic distress-call.

The plane was followed soon after by a small and swift boat bearing a boarding party. From the bow of the craft, Clifton Storm led his party of adventurers out into the black night in search of what could be the latest victims of Poseidon's curse. In his mind, the frantic last words of the distress message replayed themselves: *"They want the ship... they want us...!"*

From the air, the Aegean Sea was a vast and impenetrable table of blackness. Diana and her gunner scanned the waves as they got closer to the area from where the signal had originated. Their eyes were met only met with darkness until at last the tiny glimmer of lights winked at them feebly from below. It was a small cargo steamer, an old rust-bucket of a ship. Circling the craft, they peered at it through the night; it seemed to be deserted, and no motion could be seen from the ship.

"We might be too late, Cliff," she called into the radio's microphone after she announced their location to Storm and his party. "This tub looks deserted."

"Keep circling, Diana, we're almost there." Storm had the boat's pilot adjust their course accordingly and he performed a last-minute gear-check. The party was outfitted with thick peacoats against the strangely chilly night, but it wasn't the temperature that iced Storm's senses on this mission. Worry gnawed at his insides, along with a tingly feeling. He wasn't sure if it was the mystery of what they were headed toward or whether it was something else. Rather than dismiss it, he held onto that feeling; sometimes his instincts helped to keep him sharp and had kept him alive on more than one occasion. His quiet energy increased, like a jungle-cat poised to strike.

When the speedy boat arrived they could see the dim glimmer of lights and could confirm what Diana had reported: nothing moved on the ship's deck, and it drifted on the dark waves with no direction and no hand to helm it. The MARDL craft heaved-to on the boat's port-side and the crew attached boarding ladders to it. Storm, Brock, and a team of five other crewmembers from the *Independence* climbed aboard and began to fan out across the deck. They began a search of the craft, Tommy guns at the ready for the first sign of trouble. Meanwhile, Diana's plane continued to circle in the dark overhead as the boarding party scoured the drifting steamer. No identification was evident so far on board—the craft didn't even have a name, it seemed. It was a nondescript ghost-ship.

The group split up and moved throughout the ship, checking the cabins, galley, store-rooms. Nothing turned up beside more emptiness. There were very few furnishings, too, as though the ship had hardly ever been occupied in the first place.

"It's all clear up here," Storm announced finally. "We're going below deck." With that, they began to file down the stairs to the next level of the small steamship.

Although she wasn't onboard the derelict with Storm, Diana St. Clair was feeling anxious for the boarding party. The eeriness of the situation was getting to her, and the long stretch of radio-silence wasn't helping. Impatiently, she checked her gauges for what seemed to be the hundredth time. She was interrupted by a tap on her shoulder as her gunner attempted to get her attention. He pointed, and she returned her eyes to the waves below: something odd was occurring. A strange fog was beginning to sprout up all around the ship. In moments, the strange mist thickened enough that she could just barely make out the glow of the crafts' lights.

Diana clicked on the plane's searchlight and swiveled it to cast its beam onto the Aegean. The strange fog blocked the light, however, and she could

A floatplane...emerged from inside the vessel...

no longer see the boats below at all. She grabbed the radio's mic. "Tyner," she called to the speedboat's pilot. "Tyner, what's going on with all that fog?"

Silence was her only answer. Diana tried to hail Tyner again; far below and within the fog, her voice crackled unheard from the speakers of the boat's radio. Tyner, a hardily-built sailor, slumped unmoving in front of the radio set. With blank and glazing eyes he sat dead, a deep and ragged wound oozing blood from his back.

Storm and his crew descended the steps and entered the boat's engine room. The throbbing boiler and engine gave the men a little comfort: obviously it had been occupied relatively recently, and this knowledge helped alleviate some of the strange feelings of isolation and abandonment that was onboard. They hoped to find someone here, some remnants of the boat's crew. They checked the chamber thoroughly and found yet again no sign of the ship's inhabitants.

After their repeated non-discoveries, they made their way at last to the final place they hadn't yet checked: the cargo hold. The door, they found, was unlocked and they steeled themselves for what they might find inside. Stepping cautiously into the hold, they found the lights weren't working in the room, and they had to resort to clicking on their flashlights.

Yellow beams feebly pierced the dusty blackness of the hold to reveal the space to be nearly empty. At the far end of the hold sat the large humped shapes of a few crates. The group made their way forward, feeling the failure of what they had hoped would be a rescue mission. They hoped that at least the crates may hold some contents, some clue of what the ship had been hauling, and maybe who the crew may have been.

A sound, faint but insistent, came to Storm's ears. He stopped, straining to hear it among the footsteps of his comrades: it was a strange, rhythmic sound; a hiss followed by an expulsion of air, accompanied by a faint gurgling. It sounded almost like breathing. If it was breathing, then it wasn't human, and it sounded as though there was more than one source to this sound.

Suddenly from around the crates hulking black shapes appeared in the struggling beams of the crews' flashlights. The dimly-seen forms crouched menacingly and raised their weapons at the crew from the *Independence*.

CHAPTER 11: SLAUGHTER ON THE HIGH SEAS

The MARDL crew was stunned by the surprise appearance of the strange shapes: humanoid but monstrous and hulking, glistening black and thorny in the dim light of their flashlight beams. The ambushers held some kind of spears, and one of these shot a strange glittering projectile. It struck Jenkins—the crew-member to Storm's right—in the chest and it knocked him backward, his chest spraying blood. The other shapes—three altogether—began to fire their weapons as well.

The rescue crew scattered under this strange weapons-fire and Storm reached beneath his heavy coat and flung an object that he plucked from. The troubleshooter almost always wore a custom-made utility-harness which held tools, gadgets, and weapons that came in handy in his adventures. It was from this that he had drawn and thrown a small concussion grenade, which sailed across the room before bouncing among the three marauders. It exploded in a thunderous burst of sound and pressure, but it only succeeded in knocking down the enemy that had been closest to the grenade. The remaining pair miraculously remained standing, though they hesitated as if stunned.

Though their ears rang, the crew from the *Independence* was ready to fight. "Open fire!" Storm called to them, and their submachine guns began chattering, a thunderous roaring that filled the cargo hold but only for a moment. Their Tommy gun bullets suddenly did the unexpected and bounced off the black skin of the things. The projectiles whined and whistled around the room, ricocheting further off the metal walls of the hold. Another crewman dropped to the ground with a shout of pain as a misdirected slug hit him in the leg. Meanwhile the invading monstrosities had recovered from the grenade and began firing their weapons anew. Another MARDL member spun around with a scream, his shoulder a ripped and bloody mess.

"Geez, we can't crack 'em!" Brock shouted to Storm, who was as stunned as his teammates. "We're getting butchered here, Cliff!"

"Fall back! Get those men and get out of here!" Storm commanded, and Brock and the remaining crew struggled to pick up their fallen comrades. The ambushing monsters were overpowering them: the things had succeeded in whittling their number from seven down to four in a matter of seconds, and so far they were seemingly unstoppable. They had to be distracted so the team could escape.

As Brock and the other two members of the party began extracting themselves and their wounded and dead friends, Storm drew another set of grenades from his harness. With both hands he flung a pair of the concussion grenades to the side of the room, and he followed them with an incendiary bomb which he tossed to the floor between him and the oncoming horrors. The concussion grenades exploded almost as one at the right side of the room, and seawater began pouring into the rupture that they had caused. The incendiary device burst and spread out a wall of flame between Storm and the shapes, and he turned and sprinted after his men without stopping to see if they were being followed. He knew the flames wouldn't last long—especially with the rushing seawater that was filling the cargo hold—and he hoped to get away from the things before they could catch up to him and his men. The things weren't going to be beaten by traditional means, and he and his crew had to regroup and escape if he was to figure out how to defeat them.

Brock and the rest of the boarding party made it back to the derelict boat's deck, stopping for just a moment to wonder at the bizarre mist that had enveloped the ship while they had been aboard. Upon arrival at the speedboat, he called out to Tyner to start up the craft's engine for their getaway and escape. There was no reply to his calls. The muscular troubleshooter slid down the boarding ladder and upon reaching the smaller boat's deck, Brock could see Tyner's body slumped at the wheel.

"Not another one…!" He said under his breath. He dragged the corpse away from the helm and started the engine, then began helping the others pass down the wounded and dead. Once they were on board, Brock went up the ladder and back onto the derelict, which was starting to list to one side, sinking from the punctured hull.

As Storm emerged from the cabin and onto the sinking vessel's deck, a flash of movement in the fog to his left caught his eye. A fourth hulking black shape was there and it lunged at him. Storm sidestepped the attacker and in a moment of clarity time seemed to slow for him. He could see the weapon of the invader: a spear-like shaft, obviously a mechanical construction of some sort, attached via a hose to the humped back of the armored shape. The attacks in the cargo hold and Doc Foster's words came back to him: "...*something punched holes into him with simple water.*" He had to know for sure.

With the attacker's armaments revealed to him, Storm drew a knife from his harness. The large and bulky armored form was slow to turn and using his momentary advantage Storm sliced through the weapon's hose. Pressurized water sprayed out and the hose flailed wildly. The spray of saltwater raked across Storm's face and he was blinded. Instinctively, he threw his hands to his face.

The attacker had regained his bearings. Realizing that the weapon was now useless, it dropped the water-spear to the deck and lunged at Storm, wrapping thick armored arms around his ribs and raising him off his feet. Storm gasped: pain gripped him and he realized he was going to be crushed. His stinging vision narrowed as he began blacking out, but as he did he gazed into the face of the thing only to find himself looking through a reinforced glass visor and into the face of another man. This was no monster from the deep; this was a man in some kind of powered suit of armor. Comprehension mixed with his struggle as his tunnel-vision closed down to a pinpoint.

Suddenly, Brock lunged from the closing darkness. Grabbing the arms of the armored killer from behind, he pulled with all his strength. Though it seemed futile at first, the man's grip on Storm lessened almost imperceptibly. Storm fought through his encroaching unconsciousness and drew an object from the harness beneath his coat. It was another concussion device, one that worked on a delayed timer and had a thick wad of strong adhesive attached to it. He slapped this to the helmet of the assassin and flicked a switch.

The attacker suddenly understood Storm's actions: he was now wearing a bomb! Though he was armored, he knew there would be some damage to him if it went off right outside his helmet. Fearing for his life, he dropped Storm to claw at the sticky-bomb. As he staggered in fear, Storm and Brock took off running back across the deck and to their craft.

As Storm stooped to pick up the attacker's fallen water-spear the bomb went off, knocking the would-be killer to the ground. Within the suit's helmet, blood had erupted from the thug's nose. He had blacked out for a moment upon the detonation. Regaining his consciousness, he shakily rose to his feet and began a weaving trot toward Storm and Brock as they began climbing down the boarding ladder. A murderous rage filled the killer as he advanced on them.

With a defiant roar, Diana's plane swooped down low through the fog and over the sinking craft. The gunner in the aircraft's turret saw the pursuing metal-man and opened fire with his weapons: a pair of M2 Browning heavy machine guns. The big slugs tore into the armored thug as the floatplane strafed him, and his armored suit became his death-shroud. He fell, first to his knees and then flat on the deck, lifeless.

Storm and Brock made it down the ladder and to their craft. Once they were aboard, the speed-craft's new pilot laid on the throttle and it shot away on the black waves, speeding away from the sinking derelict craft that had been the source of their nightmarish ambush.

Overhead, Diana banked the floatplane and looked down at the rusty steamship as it sank into the waves. One last time she swept the sea around the ship and the mysterious billowing fog with her searchlight. Behind her goggles, her sapphire eyes widened: for just a moment she could have sworn that she had seen a huge shape sliding away beneath the waves of the Aegean Sea.

CHAPTER 12:
THE PRICE OF FAILURE

fter radioing ahead to the *Independence*, the MARDL boarding crew arrived back at the home-ship to find medical crews ready in the ship's docking bay. As soon as the speedboat had been tied fast to the dock the attendants swarmed the craft and loaded the wounded onto gurneys to be bustled back to the medical bay. The corpses of the two slain party members were also bundled up to be sent to the morgue. Doc Foster and his crew would be busy this night. Clifton Storm watched with a somber face as the wounded and the dead were carted off.

Once the bay was cleared and the boat hoisted out of the water, Diana taxied her floatplane into the bay. She was wondering how her friend had been handling the experience onboard the derelict, but Storm had disappeared by the time she disembarked from the plane.

"Brock," she queried of the big troubleshooter as he assisted the dock crew with hoisting the plane into the maintenance bay, "what happened down there? Where's Cliff?"

Brock relayed the incident onboard to her. After the tale was done, he turned to Diana. "Cliff's off to see Willy about the weapon he grabbed… then I think he wants to be alone for now. I don't think he's taking this too well… give him some room for a while. Don't take that the wrong way, but I know Cliff. He shuts off at times like this, and it's best to just let him be alone for the time being."

She nodded sadly in concern for her friend, and the two of them went off to grab some coffee to warm up and try to shake off the chilly and deadly night.

Willy Avis was woken up by Storm, who apologized profusely. "I really need you on this one, Willy," he said as he handed the mechanical genius the weapon. "Take a good look at this." The mechanic brought the weapon to the lamp in his cabin. His eyes, originally squinting in his half-asleep state, slowly opened wider as he examined it. "Where'd you get this?" he said finally.

Storm told Willy of the derelict and the S.O.S., of the ambush and the tragedies onboard and of the narrow escape from the armored enemies.

"Do you think you can tinker with this thing enough to see how it works? We need to know what we're dealing with here."

"Yeah," the older man nodded. He ran a hand through his salt and pepper hair and put on a pair of glasses, then looked up at Storm. It was the first time he'd noticed how tired and ragged his friend and boss looked. Storm's eyes, usually full of energy and vitality, looked like empty holes. "Cliff, you look like hell."

Storm nodded. "I suppose I do…. Look, in the morning I'm gonna brief everyone on tonight's events and what we know so far about what we're up against. I really appreciate your help with this. I need to get back to my cabin for a while and think things through. I'll swing by later and see what you've got here. Thanks, Willy."

Storm left the room and shut the door behind him. The mechanic stood by his desk and looked at the closed door for a while. Willy was a combat veteran; he had seen a lot in his time, and realized that his friend may be experiencing things that had been a part of his own life for a long time. They were new experiences for Storm, and if he was to continue with his mission he'd have to learn to deal with them. Willy sighed and turned back to the strange device on his desk.

After closing the door to his own quarters, Storm showered and changed into dry clothes. Doom seemed to cling to him: he had dealt death before in his adventures and missions against those who would harm the innocent, but this was the first time he'd ever experienced death on his own side. Two people had died tonight under his command, and two more were injured and in critical care down in the *Independence*'s medical bay. Storm had led the party aboard the derelict and perhaps, he felt, this was his own entire fault. If he'd only been more cautious or better prepared, or maybe he'd been foolish to even attempt a rescue mission in the way he had. He looked down at the white shirt he'd taken off a few moments before and realized for the first time that it was covered in the blood of his teammates….

Storm sat down behind his desk in the dark cabin. He was fatigued, bewildered and harried. He knew he needed rest, but couldn't stop his mind from thinking, re-planning and strategizing the rescue…. He couldn't stop thinking about how he'd failed his men.

Jimmy, the lanky gangster, led rat-faced Oakley and the gorilla-like

Packer through the tunnels of Poseidon's hidden base of operations. The fear and trepidation the group felt the last time they reported to their leader was stronger now. Not only had they failed again in their attempt to eliminate Challenger Storm, but they were coming back now with one fewer member of their group; in their armor the trio had been the ones to ambush the troubleshooters in the cargo hold, and after being surprised by Storm's grenades and his swift retreat they had escaped the derelict through the hole that had been torn in the side of the ship. They had surfaced just in time to have seen Fitz gunned down by the MARDL plane as he pursued Storm and Brock across the deck. The three thugs had managed to remove Fitz's body from the wreckage as it sank and had brought it back to the cave-base with them.

Once again standing before Poseidon in his throne room, the group nearly trembled in fear. Poseidon, however, calmly remained seated as they told of their failure to him: much of the news had already been reported to him by others but this was their official version. Once they were done, he remained quiet, his face in shadow. Long moments stretched into minutes, and the three were beginning to wonder if their boss was asleep....

"They told me that Fitz was missing his weapon," he said at last. His voice was low and ominous. "They've told me that it looks like it was cut off from its conduit tubing. Do you know what this means?"

The thugs looked at one another, puzzled.

"It means," Poseidon continued, "that Storm possibly now has it in his possession. Between his experience with us tonight and one of our weapons in his hands, some of our secrets are exposed. We have now probably lost the edge of our 'curse' angle. No longer are our methods considered 'supernatural.' This forces me to change my plans." He raised his head to look at them, and one of his eyes caught the light, giving his darkened face a touch of the demonic. "I don't like to change my plans unless I am ready to do so."

The trio froze. Oakley and Packer were silent, their tongues sandpaper inside their mouths. Jimmy, however, began stammering. He was the group's leader out in the field and all of them knew the failure of the group, though not a solitary fault, rested on his shoulders.

"Aw, look boss, I tried—*we* tried to get 'em," he gibbered, "they reacted really fast, though. Even with all the lead flyin' around in there and our spears goin' at 'em full-blast, that Storm guy kept his cool, and got 'em all out of there before we could get closer to 'em. I dunno where Fitz was, but he was late, if he'd been faster he'd have gotten 'em pinned in there with us. I dunno how the hell they got…"

"Enough," Poseidon commanded, and Jimmy's mouth promptly snapped shut. "I warned you, Jimmy, and I know you know the price of your failure to carry out my orders to the letter. Oakley, Packer: you are relieved of your duty for now. Go back to your quarters and think long and hard about my views toward failure."

Poseidon waved his hand in a vague signal and Jimmy began to sweat as a pair of Poseidon's minions appeared from the shadows on either side of the throne room. Like Herbert Chalmers, they were glassy-eyed robotic servants that populated much of Poseidon's secret empire. They grabbed the lanky gangster by the arms securely and he silently pleaded to Oakley and Packer with his eyes.

Jimmy's allies were helpless in the face and rule of Poseidon. After quick looks of sympathy, they averted their eyes from Jimmy's and left through the throne room's massive iron door. The mindless pair of servants led Jimmy away through another, secret door off to the side of the throne room's stairs. Poseidon followed them through the door, accompanying Jimmy to his fate.

CHAPTER 13: THE ENEMY REVEALED

The sunrise over the Aegean Sea found a very tired and unshaven Clifton Storm sitting at the desk where he'd been sitting for the remainder of his black night. He had been unable to get any sleep and spent most of the dark hours contemplating the nature of his mission and his place as a leader. The men who died had known the perils and dangers of the quest that Storm was spearheading, the mission of bringing justice to the innocent, when they had signed on to work with MARDL. They knew this just as surely as policemen, firemen, and members of the military knew the risks of their own jobs. Even though he knew they were prepared to face this fate and his repeated attempts at rationalization, Storm still couldn't help but feel guilty for leading them into battle. With bleary eyes and a heavy sigh, Storm pulled the files of the dead men and updated them, ending this action with the penning of letters to the men's families. He had been dreading this last, finalizing act. It was the hardest step during Storm's night, and completing the action brought him a fresh wave of guilt.

The letters completed and the files closed, Storm sat back and sipped another cup of coffee and stared out at the water and the blazing disk of the sun as it crept over the horizon. Doc Foster had contacted him using the intercom on Storm's desk: he was thankful to learn that neither of the wounded men had passed away during the night and their conditions were now stable. This was relieving news to the adventurer, who took solace in the fact that the death-count could have been worse.

Storm's reverie was interrupted by a knock at the door. He pressed a button beneath his desk that unlocked the door to his quarters. "Come in," he called, and he was surprised at the gravelly tone in his voice.

Diana St. Clair entered the unlocked door. In her crisp white shirt and loose black trousers, she looked every bit as fresh and bright as Storm felt tired and grungy. She halted several steps into the office and looked around. "Geez, Cliff…"

"I know, I know. I look like hell," he interrupted. "Willy told me so last night, and I don't feel any better now. I didn't get an ounce of sleep."

The aviatrix smiled. "No, I was going to say: 'Geez, Cliff, this place looks as bad as your office did back at home.'" Her smile softened into a look of concern. "How are you holding up?"

Storm shrugged and looked back out the window at the sunrise. "About as good as a guy can be after writing condolence letters to loved ones. I'm going to be hated, Diana. I'm sending a flyer to the mainland later today, and those letters will go back around to the other side of the world soon. And when those mothers and fathers and girlfriends and siblings get those letters, they're going to hate me for getting their special people tossed into a meat grinder."

Diana sat on Storm's desk and laid her hand atop his. He looked at it.

"Don't hate yourself, Cliff. They knew what they were getting into. It's not your fault, and if you let this eat at you you're not going to be any good to anybody out here. Nobody blames you. Just let it go."

He looked at her and nodded silently, sadly.

The *Independence* had its own large meeting room; it was dubbed "the auditorium" but it was nowhere near so grand as its nickname would lead one to believe. About an hour after the scene in Storm's office, most of the seagoing MARDL personnel began to file into the auditorium and sat down in its chairs amid a murmur of conversation. By now the news had spread throughout the big ship: Clifton Storm and an away-team had encountered something out in the ocean and it nearly got the better of all of its members. The excitement, mystery, and deadly seriousness of "the Poseidon's curse affair" were growing, and everyone was eager to hear more details about the confirmed first contact with the enemy.

On the auditorium's "stage"—essentially just a raised platform at the head of the room—several humped shapes sat hidden under tarpaulins. Willy Avis, who had been up since Storm presented him with his strange find, was on this platform and tinkering with the shapes. He was older than most of the members of Storm's organization who saw action out in the field, but he was very energetic and fit for his age. Well liked by his MARDL teammates, Willy was very welcome on missions for both his mechanical and combat expertise alike.

The murmuring voices died down as Clifton Storm himself entered into the auditorium, along with Brock Thurston and Diana St. Clair. Storm still was tired and felt hollow, but he had shaved his face and had assumed the air of authority once again. He stood in front of the stage and began the meeting.

"Okay, folks, I'm sure everyone has heard at least some version of what happened last night so I want to set the record straight. Shortly after midnight we intercepted an S.O.S. signal from an unidentified craft. The sender of the message led us to believe that they were under siege from an unknown group of assailants who wanted the ship and its crew for an unspecified reason. We scrambled an advance air support as well as a boarding party to meet the ship, which I myself led. Upon arriving at the derelict, no signs of life were evident and so the party and I boarded the ship. Shortly thereafter Diana, our air support pilot, and her gunner noted a sudden and dense patch of fog or mist sprout up around the ship and completely cutting it off from visual contact. Diana attempted to hail our intercept boat but was unsuccessful. We learned later that before or during this time Tyner Archer, who was at the helm, had unfortunately been killed."

Storm cleared his throat and continued. "Meanwhile aboard the vessel the boarding party and I discovered there was nobody home. No signs of habitation, even recent signs, cigarette butts, et cetera, were found aboard. Our search led us throughout the ship and finally to the cargo hold, where we were confronted by three unknown assailants wearing some kind of heavily armored suits of unknown purpose and origin." At this, Storm turned to a large pad of paper, onto which he had drawn a sketch of the mysterious suits. He pulled back the cover of the pad and revealed his sketches of the enemy's armor.

"After they fired on us," Storm continued, "the team and I engaged in a battle with the three individuals. Our bullets did little or no damage to the suits, and instead bounced and ricocheted off their surface. We had to beat a retreat from them, since we were obviously under-gunned. During this shootout, the assailants also claimed the life of another boarding party member, Leroy Jenkins, while two other members of the group, Bell and Yuris, were wounded and are now recovering in the sickbay. Evidently, these suits also give the wearer an increased amount of strength. I learned this when a fourth attacker accosted me on deck on my way out and I came close to being a pancake. Thanks to Brock's intervention and the higher caliber of bullets fired from our air support that particular attempted murderer is no longer among the living."

Storm looked around the room. "These folks are serious, gang. I can't guess at their motives yet, though I think I may have an idea about who might be behind it all. Whoever they are, these pirates are dangerous and are more than heavily armed and I don't want to lose any more people out here.

He...revealed his sketches of the enemy's armor.

"Now," Storm said as he hopped nimbly up onto the stage platform, "we've come to the show-and-tell portion of this morning's meeting." He and Willy began to pull the coverings off of the shapes on the stage, and these were revealed to be an upright sheet of steel at stage right, and a large machine on the opposite side.

"During my combat with the last of our friends last night, I managed to relieve him of his weapon." At this he pointed to the drawing of the armored marauder, specifically to the spear-like weapon and its feeder-tube. "It was, I believe, this kind of weapon that caused the damages to the body that was found floating in the sea by those tourists yesterday, and to the bodies of Tyner and Jenkins on board the derelict. Willy." Storm finished with a wave to the mechanic, who took over the demonstration.

"What we've got here," Willy began, "is some kind of advanced high-pressure water nozzle. Since whoever's behind all this is trying to create superstition with this 'Poseidon' nonsense, I'm assuming they designed this weapon to lend mystery to the whole thing. Think of it as a souped-up version of your standard garden hose." He held up the weapon for the group to see. "This is it. Doesn't look like much, I know. We've got it hooked up to one of our surplus bilge pumps here, since it's the closest thing we could find to whatever technology they've got built into their suits. Whatever they're using, it's very compact and advanced, and it's able to fit into the back of their bulletproof getups."

Willy turned on the pump, which began running loudly, and he and Storm donned pairs of thick goggles. Bracing himself, Willy pointed the water-spear at the sheet of steel and pressed the firing stud. There was a brief, loud hiss. The weapon's kick was surprisingly strong and staggered the mechanic backward, but the burst of water sped true: striking the target with a loud "kerrang!" the water punched a hole in the steel sheet. For effect, Willy used the weapon several more times and punched three more holes into the steel target. He turned off the pump and silence reigned in the auditorium.

Storm pulled his goggles down around his neck. "That's simple water, folks. These pirates are dangerous: they're heavily armored and out here there's no shortage of ammunition for them."

The day shift radio operator burst through the auditorium doors, red faced and out of breath. He had run from the bridge to the meeting room as fast as he'd been able.

"It's Poseidon..." he gulped. "He's at it again and this time he's gone public!"

CHAPTER 14: "THE CHARADE IS OVER."

I n the radio room of the *Independence* Clifton Storm, Captain Horne, and about a dozen other members of the MARDL ship crowded around the speakers. Issuing forth from the radio set was the voice of Poseidon; the voice was augmented with some kind of modulator and sounded unearthly, and was imperious as it threatened its audience.

"Once again," Poseidon's voice boomed and hissed. "To all those within the sound of my voice: I come to you now revealed, a very real and physical threat. For too long I have been attacking and stealing ships in the night, testing my powers and amassing my army. That is now the past, the charade is over. I, Poseidon, lord of the seas, announce to you my intentions. Soon, members of the Grecian government will receive my demands of a certain amount of money to be paid in tribute to me, by certain means and on a fixed and inflexible schedule. Once these demands have been received, they will be on this schedule permanently. If these tributary payments are not made completely and promptly and on time, I shall destroy a coastal city every day until the demands are met. This action will also extend toward any seagoing vessels as well, resulting in a total lockdown of the Aegean Sea and of the maritime industry upon which the area thrives." Here Poseidon laughed, a strange, grating sound filtered through the voice modulator. "A word of warning: do not try to find me; your efforts will fail. At the conclusion of this message, the broadcasting tower that is sending it out will self destruct upon its tiny island in the sea and any efforts to trace it back to my home location will prove fruitless. I understand that the incredible size of my boast may lead many to doubt my power, and so to prove my might I will, at the stroke of five p.m. today, unleash a wave of substantial force upon the coastal town of Limenas Thasou on the island of Thasos."

This announcement set off a wave of astonished exclamations from the group in the radio room. "Quiet!" Storm barked, as they had momentarily drowned out Poseidon's voice. The din fell as soon as it rose.

"I am not normally a charitable man, but in this case I am giving the people of Limenas Thasou a chance to evacuate before I demonstrate my power. You would be wise to take advantage of this chance, because— make no mistake—I *will* strike the city today. I know that certain forces will be on hand to try to confront me, whether it is the Grecian military or the independent meddlers from the United States. You will most assuredly not be able to stop me but are welcome to try.

"And so," the voice went on, "I conclude this message with a final warning to those in power: do not disobey these orders once you have received them, and *do not take my threat lightly*. Poseidon demands tribute or will extract payment from the blood of the drowned and disobedient. You have until exactly five o'clock today to evacuate Limenas Thasou. Good day."

With those final words, there was a burst of static noise and a piercing squelch from the radio speakers, followed by a softer static and then silence. Somewhere out in the sea, the broadcasting tower had destroyed itself in a series of explosions. Poseidon had been true to his words.

There was never any question in the minds of the crew of the *Independence*: before Storm gave the order they all knew they would be setting off toward Thasos as soon as possible. They were a good distance away and to the southeast of the island, but there would be no trouble reaching the area before the announced hour of Poseidon's attack.

Storm had learned his lesson from the encounter on board the derelict steamer and made arrangements to have the heaviest weapons at his team's disposal ready for action. Despite Poseidon's bold assurance that seekers would not find him, it was best if the troubleshooters were prepared to meet his forces if they indeed did locate them. There were a number of heavy caliber machine guns and rifles on board the ship, but there weren't enough to go around to everyone. There was another option, though: about a month before, Storm's ballistics team in Miami had been working on a kind of explosive bullet used for armor piercing needs and they had begun to produce some working prototypes. Under Storm's direction, the gunsmiths in the *Independence*'s armory now began producing the explosive ammunition for use in the field. However, due to the scarcity of the required materials aboard only a limited amount of the special rounds could be produced, and since .45 caliber handguns were the favored sidearm of most of the personnel the rounds were produced to be loaded into those weapons.

Despite their heavier arms and fortified ammunition, the team still felt on edge. Somewhere out in the sea, their quarry waited while casting its eye and its tentacles toward Thasos. The MARDL team hoped somehow to head off the enemy before it reached its target.

They had no way of knowing Poseidon had turned the table on them.

As the announced time of the wave attack drew nearer, the *Independence* was about fifty miles southeast of Thasos and passing the island of Limnos when a sudden anomaly forced them to slow their racing engines. At the lookout's sudden call, Captain Horne ordered a full stop from the engine room and used the ship's loudspeaker and intercom to summon Clifton Storm.

Several minutes later, the adventurers' leader arrived on the ship's bridge; he was still clad in the heavy apron and safety goggles he'd been wearing down in the armory's workshop. "What's going on, Cap'n?" he asked. Horne didn't utter a reply and simply pointed ahead. Storm gazed out the bridge's fore window and at the warm sea, which had been calm and serene all day long.

So far as they could see, the waves ahead of the *Independence* were now littered with icebergs. Storm knew that despite the appearance of the white slab-like shapes, these were not actually icebergs; these obstructions were no doubt more of the strange white synthetic material upon which the *Fair Game* had found the floating body of Robert Culver.

After several moments in thought, Storm turned to Horne. "We've got to go on ahead, Captain. I'd say we're making good time here, so at your discretion I'd say we need to go forward half speed. Have some of your men posted as lookouts so we can get through this mess and get to Thasos. I'm going to alert the team something's going on here and we need to be careful." Horne nodded and Storm turned to the intercom and began issuing orders.

The *Independence* forged ahead through the littered sea. Despite their best efforts they had to slow the ship yet again as the number of synthetic icebergs increased. The danger to the hull of the ship grew with each passing obstruction and the eeriness of the surroundings began to weigh upon the crew.

At Storm's command, the more combat active members of the crew began posting themselves as lookouts, scanning the sea for ships. It was possible that Poseidon was hunting them, and they had to stay on their toes. As a precaution, they had been issued an extremely limited number of the experimental explosive bullets. These were to be used as sparingly and accurately as possible by the team.

Diana St. Clair was at her perch with a heavy rifle when a sudden memory struck her: the sight of the shape just beneath the dark water on the previous night's incident with the derelict. Leaping up from her spot, she ran to where Storm was distributing the ammunition.

"Cliff, I forgot to tell you something last night," she said breathlessly as she reached him. "I'm so sorry; I meant to mention it to you. I thought it was a trick of the light, or maybe I was seeing things so I wasn't sure if I should."

"It's okay," Storm interrupted her, trying to calm her panic. "It's all right, Diana. What is it?"

"Poseidon," she gulped. "I think he's using a submarine!"

Storm's eyes grew larger. "Are you sure?"

Diana nodded. "I saw something last night, as we were leaving the sinking derelict. Something beneath the water. I wasn't sure."

Suddenly from the deck below them there was a splash and a shout and something could be glimpsed shooting into the air. There was another splash and something rocketed up out of the water again at another spot, and yet another from a different spot, and more. At the spot of each commotion, a dark shape arced through the air at the end of a plume of white water and landed upon the deck. From all directions there were more splashes and more of the objects struck the deck. Gunfire began erupting as the shapes stood up after landing and began to invade the MARDL ship. It was Poseidon's armored hordes, and all around the ship they were launching from the water and onto the deck of the *Independence*.

"It's an attack! We're being boarded!"

CHAPTER 15: THE BATTLE OF THE INDEPENDENCE

All around the massive research and exploration craft, dozens of hulking black figures were launching themselves high out of the water and up onto the deck of the *Independence*. As they had done with the *Arapaho* and the other boats they had commandeered, the armor-suited warriors of Poseidon were using unknown methods of propulsion to take themselves onto the ship and were taking the MARDL crew by surprise. Instantly, the shooting began as the heroic crew tried to stave off the attack. To a distant observer it would have sounded like a one-sided war: the weapons of the attackers made almost no noise while the crew's gunshots boomed out as they retaliated. The deadly water-spears punched holes in men and metal, however, and those targets that weren't quick or lucky were being struck down one by one.

As soon as the onslaught began, Clifton Storm dashed off to take part in the retaliation, while Diana St. Clair climbed up the nearby radio tower. Near this position, Willy Avis had taken up a spot in a makeshift machine gun turret and was already firing down upon the deck-bound invaders. From Diana's vantage point near the top of the radio tower, her sharpshooting skills would make her an ideal choice for laying down cover-fire and for sniping at the enemy agents. The rifle she was using was a German-made anti-tank rifle that had been developed during the Great War: a Mauser T-Gewehr. The bolt-action rifle fired 13-millimeter armor-piercing rounds and, they hoped, would be able to put a stop to the heavily fortified suits of the invaders.

Diana braced her back against the steel piping behind her and drew her aim on her first target as it leaped up from the water and set down on the deck near the ship's bridge. Centering her aim on the pirate's back, she pulled the trigger and nearly gasped in shock as the gun kicked in her grip. Even with the padded modifications the MARDL gunsmiths had made to the rifle's butt, the recoil against her shoulder was incredible. Her shot had been true, however, and her target fell, a spray of pressurized water jetting from the hole in the armor.

A thought made Diana hesitate before scanning for her next target: what if Herbert Chalmers was down there? She had to know why he was with Poseidon's team, if she could. Herbert was gentle, quiet and bookish, and would never be a part of this piracy; or could he? And how could she take aim at these attackers for sure if he was among them? Perhaps the target she had just brought down near the bridge had been him?

The roar and clatter of Willy's heavy machine gun turret snapped Diana out of her brief reverie. She shook her head and steeled her resolve, even though she could feel the threat of confused tears in the corners of her eyes. Below her, another black armored thug was advancing on a crewmember's unsuspecting back. Her duty to her teammates would have to come first, even though she hated herself for it. She took her aim and fired.

Storm raced across the gangway and down the stairs to the deck below. As he ran, he drew his Colt .45. Normally, Storm would have gone for his preferred pistol: the Mauser C96 Schnellfeuer with detachable magazine that always lay holstered in his utility harness. The thick armor of the pirates called for the explosive rounds, however, and so he carried the automatic pistol as well. The Colt's clip was loaded with seven of the specialty rounds and he had one extra magazine as well. That was all the explosive rounds he had for now, and he knew he'd have to conserve them and make them count. As before, he also had other tricks up his sleeves.

To his left, movement caught his eye. He leaned over a railing and gazed down, eyes growing in shock: one of the armored pirates was using a grappling device and was hanging onto the side of the ship. In the pirate's hands was some kind of device: a bomb.

Drawing a bead on the attacker from above, Storm squeezed off a shot from the .45. The bullet struck home on the pirate's helmet and it promptly blossomed into a ball of flame. Suddenly limp, the body released itself to fall back down into the waves below, the explosive sinking along with it.

A young crewmember was running past Storm, and the adventurer grabbed his arm. "Spread the word, tell everyone you can: this attack is a distraction, they're trying to set bombs on the hull. We've got to repel them!"

The crewmember nodded and sprinted away as Storm ran in the opposite direction. He grabbed the first intercom he could and switched it to the broadcast setting.

Word spread rapidly of the pirate's sabotage, not so much because of Storm's announcement over the loudspeakers or the word-of-mouth between crewmembers, but because of a thunderous explosion that shook the *Independence*'s portside.

The deck trembled from the explosion, and a quick glance confirmed the worst: an explosive had been planted and had torn a hole in the ship's hull. It was at the waterline, and seawater was rapidly pouring into the massive ship.

Inside, the crews were hurriedly evacuating the bombed section of the ship and sealing the water tight doors and shutters within. Already the water was waist deep; the partitions wouldn't stop the flooding from continuing, but they would keep it from spreading.

On the outside of the ship, the situation was worsening: more and more armored troops of Poseidon were overrunning it, providing a distraction for the MARDL crew and making it harder for them to protect the ship's hull. Storm began to coordinate a strategy: those crewmembers with heavy rifles were dispatched to key points on the deck where they could watch over the ship's hull and snipe the bombers as they attempted to set their lethal charges. Meanwhile, each sniper was protected by a ring of defenders who tried to ensure that none of the boarders would eliminate them. It was up to the remaining defenders to find and stop any boarders who made it up onto the deck.

From their high perches, Diana, Willy, and another crewmember were doing their best to pick off the invaders on the decks. Diana's brow was beaded with sweat and the right side of her chest and shoulder were bruised and sore from the repeated recoiling of the T-Gewehr rifle. She wondered how much longer the attack would go on. The pirate's attack seemed to be lessening, but this had happened a few times before and would always continue again with more ferocity.

Diana felt a slight vibration against the radio tower in which she perched. Glancing down, her eyes widened as she spotted a black armored form at the tower's base. The pirate had somehow gotten aboard and was doing something at the bottom of her perch. She gave a shout; it was a bomb he was planting there, hoping to cripple the *Independence*'s communications.

Below, the pirate's helmeted head swiveled up as he heard her cry. He had finished setting the bomb and he now raised his water spear and fired, a jet of the highly pressurized seawater speeding toward his target before she could aim her own weapon. Diana ducked back just in time, the deadly stream barely missing her head. This shot had been a diversion, though: the pirate leaped down to the deck below and jogged away seconds before the bomb went off with a deafening roar.

The radio tower shook and groaned, and Diana realized with a queasy shudder that it was leaning now, falling over toward the ship's fore section. She couldn't go anywhere and was trapped over a hundred feet up; she was riding the falling tower down to her doom.

Brock Thurman suddenly appeared below her, running beneath the collapsing tower. He called out to her and she only had a split second to leap from her spot on the tower and down into his arms. He set her on her feet and then she was running alongside him along the deck as the crashing radio tower bore down on their backs. On their left, a gap opened in the guardrail and the two of them leaped down to the lower deck below just as the twisting radio tower smashed into the spot they had been only moments before.

At that moment, Storm was dragging a severely wounded crewmember out of harm's way. He had stumbled across the bleeding and unconscious man amidst the chaos near the bow of the *Independence*. As he hauled the crewman through a door to the ship's interior, an armored pirate appeared on the deck before them and leveled his water spear at the adventurer.

Storm whipped up his pistol and fired: the first shot went wide, but the second struck the would-be murderer in the shoulder. The explosion staggered the invader backward and turned his left arm into a mangled mass of flesh and steel, but the man inside the suit grimly recovered and aimed his own weapon with one hand at Storm. The adventurer began to pull the trigger, suddenly realizing the .45's slide was jacked back. His pistol's clip, containing the last of his explosive rounds, was empty.

Suddenly the glass visor of the pirate's helmet exploded and he collapsed onto the deck. Storm looked up to see Captain Horne leaning over the deck, a rifle in his hands. He nodded at Storm and raised his weapon to his shoulder as he aimed for another intruder further up the deck.

Storm took the chance to get the wounded sailor into the ship's interior, where Doc Foster's medical staff was busy attending to the wounded or rushing the more seriously injured to the medical bay. After leaving the wounded man with attendants, Storm rushed back outside and into the battle.

Both sides were losing people but something had to be done to gain the upper hand, something to keep the invaders at bay. Storm had observed that the pirates would often leap back into the water and reboard the *Independence* moments later; he reasoned that this was how they were refilling the water reservoirs for their spear weapons. If only something could hold them in the water, or prevent those on the ship from returning to the water or their submarine…. In thought, Storm adjusted his utility harness and his hand brushed one of his ensnaring tangle grenades. A thought hit him, crazy but entirely possible.

Rushing back inside and to an intercom, he connected to the operations center. Gibb, the docking and launch specialist, picked up. Storm gave his order and then returned to the deck and to the conflict.

Moments later, massive mechanical pulley systems on either side of the *Independence* swung into action and into position. From these, pneumatic jets launched massive dragnets out and into the water on either side of the MARDL ship. As the oceangoing mobile base of the Miami Aerodrome Research & Development Labs, the ship was outfitted with a full comp-lement of scientific study equipment. The nets were used to dredge the ocean for sealife or for debris that could be hauled aboard during salvage operations. A thick and tightly woven net of steel-strong fibers spread out over the waves around the boat, ensnaring those of Poseidon's combatants that were in the water and preventing them from boarding the ship again.

Meanwhile, those pirates left aboard were quickly outgunned and overrun. Without water to fuel their spear-like weapons, they had to rely on brute augmented strength for hand-to-hand combat, and they knew that would only last for a short while until they were either gunned down or outnumbered. The pirates suddenly faced defeat.

Oakley, the lieutenant of Poseidon with the rat-like face, cursed loudly within his suit of powered steel armor. The attack had been a failure. They had intended on overrunning the ship and taking the crew hostage while crippling the *Independence* with their hull bombs, but they hadn't counted on Storm's crew fighting back so strongly. They'd underestimated the troubleshooters and now they were going to have to run.

"Get outta here, retreat!" he called to his comrades over their communications systems. He next addressed the sub waiting below them: "*Athena*, prepare to receive all divers. Get a Hammer ready to hit this tub; I have a feeling we're gonna have to cover our tracks a little."

"This is *Athena*; orders received," replied a voice in his headset.

Oakley turned to leave via the nearest railing and found himself face to face with Challenger Storm himself as he was rounding a nearby corner. The adventurer was as shocked as the gangster at this unexpected meeting, but Oakley reacted quickly.

Oakley swung his fist at the scarred face of Clifton Storm, who ducked and sidestepped and began reaching for one of his gadgets.

"Not this time!" thought the pirate of Poseidon, and he threw a rapid jab at Storm's head.

The mechanically aided blow only grazed Storm's skull. If it had fully connected it would have killed him, but it still had an effect. The troubleshooter's vision swam with stars and a black veil seemed to fall around him and the world. With a groan Storm crumpled to the deck, unconscious.

Oakley looked around quickly: in the distance, only one person could be seen in the immediate area, a dark haired beauty holding a rifle. Oakley recalled tangling with the same woman when they were on F.P. 1. She was a sharpshooter, and no doubt could drop him from here with a well placed shot. She saw him and dropped into a kneeling position as she took aim. Oakley hurriedly picked up the unconscious form at his feet. Throwing Storm over his shoulder, he leaped over the railing and into the water below. From her position Diana swore and began running to the spot where the pirate and Storm had disappeared.

On the surface below, Oakley detached an emergency oxygen tank with breather mask from his leg armor and strapped it quickly to Storm. Securing the mask to Storm's face, he opened the valve on the tank and dove underwater with his captive, just as Diana arrived at the railing. A trail of bubbles on the water's surface was all that was left of them when she got there.

Below the waves Oakley dove down, pulling his limp hostage behind him. Through the clear blue water Oakley could see Poseidon's sub, the *Athena*, waiting just below, its airlocks open. Swimming into the nearest airlock chamber, the gangster pulled the outer door shut behind him and secured it.

Once again he radioed his comrades aboard the sub. *"Athena*, this is Oakley. I'm aboard. Is everyone accounted for?"

"Everyone that can be," replied the radio operator. "And the Hammer is ready."

"Good, then hit 'em hard with it once and reel it back in, and then let's get the hell out of here."

"Roger that, Oakley, we're ringing their bell right now!"

Oakley grinned evilly as he activated the airlock's bilge pumps. He looked to the opposite side of the airlock's chamber. There, unconscious and slumped in the corner, Clifton Storm was oblivious behind his oxygen mask.

Down below the sub a strange mechanism sat on the seabed, connected to the *Athena* by a tether. It rumbled to life as complex machinery activated inside its rounded exterior. There was a throbbing noise that rose to a whining sound, and then a single dull booming thud that rippled the silt around it.

On board the *Independence*, there was confusion as word spread that the team's leader had been taken hostage. The launch operations center had been alerted and was readying the MARDL submersible for pursuit when the weird boom rattled the hull of the ship. The launch crew looked at each other with puzzled expressions.

On the deck, a search party was being assembled to give chase in the sub when they felt the vibrations. Something was happening. The sea was trembling.

There was a shout and someone pointed, and all eyes turned to follow their lead. What faced them was terrible, like a monster out of legend. On the ship's bridge someone saw it and slapped the toggle for the alarm, which began whooping frantically.

Rising up to broadside the *Independence* was a massive wave. It seemed to curl over the ship like a cobra about to strike before it finally fell upon the ship.

CHAPTER 16: BROKEN

The adventurers had little time to react to the freak wave. They scrambled frantically for something to hold onto before the wall of water crashed down upon the *Independence*. Those on the decks who couldn't find something to hold onto mostly clung to the others who did. A few of the other crewmembers weren't so lucky.

The monstrous and foaming green wave slammed down upon the *Independence* with an incredible force, like a massive sledgehammer wielded by an ancient and powerful god that threatened to drown all those below it. Following the hellish blow the sea beneath the ship swelled and pitched violently, turning the *Independence* on its side and pushing it; the cataclysmic eruption of water threatened to capsize the MARDL ship completely. Within the ship people, furniture, and equipment were violently thrown around like trash in a windstorm.

Providence saved the craft from being turned over all the way: as the ship rode the wave it crashed into one of the largest of Poseidon's synthetic "ice bergs" that had littered the sea around the *Independence*. Though it served to crush the ship's opposite side somewhat, the huge white block managed to prop up the ship and kept it from rolling over.

As the sea behind the wave dropped back down, so too did the *Independence* roll back onto an even keel, providing yet another shocking crash and tremor throughout the entire ship.

The rippling sea eventually calmed down. The danger had passed and the MARDL team began to spring into action once more.

A number of those on the *Independence*'s decks had been washed overboard by the waves, and crews now scrambled to man the lifeboats to search for them or the bodies of those who didn't make it. The boats were lowered in a hurry and the sailors aboard them began rowing toward the bodies and survivors that could be seen. The wave had thrown debris and sailors far and wide, and a few flares popped up into the air in the distance from those who had been washed far away.

On the deck, Captain Horne began to call for damage reports from all hands. The power had been knocked out of the *Independence* and word had to be passed from man to man. As the reports started to pour in, the situation began to look worse by the second. The weathered Captain's face began to change from concerned to grave to hopeless. The *Independence* was crippled and without power and communications, with heavy damages from all sectors of the ship. The injuries and casualties were piling up. They were dead in the water.

After seeing to the injured in their area Willy, Diana, and Brock convened along with some of the other higher ranking members of Storm's troubleshooters in a supply room; while the ship and its crew were being seen to by Horne and his team, they were meeting to plan their strategy for the search for their leader.

Storm was gone, taken by one of the pirates. There was no doubt that Poseidon's forces had run away after their defeat. The wave that struck the ship was enough to give the *Independence* plenty to worry about while the pirates got away with their prize captive.

"We've got to comb this area for him," Brock urged the others. "They can't have gotten that far yet, right?"

"We don't know that," Willy countered. "These guys have got some weird science on their side. We've only seen a fraction of their equipment in action. They could be miles from here by now."

"Look, we won't know until we try," Diana put in. "I say while we lick our wounds here, we get everything we've got out there: planes, boats, and the sub. Hell, even the lifeboats can get out there looking. We're losing time."

Willy lit a cigarette and scowled. "I'm with you, Diana, I really am, but have you heard the reports from the launch bay lately? Everything is pretty banged up down there. There's no way in hell we can scramble out there now. We're in a bad way and we're not going anywhere anytime soon."

Diana bit her lip and turned away. Brock punched a metal storage locker in frustration. They were powerless.

It was dark. He was wet and shivering. For a moment, the memory of an icy night on a mountainside came back to him, the smell of burning fuel and the feeling of blood oozing down his face.

Storm's eyes snapped open and darted around. Reality came back to him as his grogginess receded. He wasn't on the mountain: that was years ago, though the memory still haunted him sometimes, but now he was here. But where the hell was here?

...the situation began to look worse by the second.

He was in a small chamber of some kind, alone; a cell. Storm sat up and realized that he must be aboard a ship of some kind: there was a slight feeling of motion. His wrists were shackled in front of him, as were his ankles. Apart from the throbbing in his head from the blow that had knocked him out, he was unharmed. There was a single light bulb set into the ceiling behind a metal cage, and its light was very dim. The walls were metal; Storm probed at them but couldn't seem to find any kind of crack or separation in them that would indicate a door. Next, his hands played over the shackles in search of a keyhole. He was surprised to find none.

He reached for his utility harness, though he knew what he would probably find. As expected, the multi-pocketed leather gear was gone. The tools, gadgets, and weapons that it housed weren't there for him, but he wasn't completely without tools.

Storm reached down to his right ankle. There, strapped against his skin beneath his boot and sock, was a small glass vial within a padded sheath. Storm slid the vial out and palmed it the way a magician would palm a coin. He smiled grimly to himself. Now, all that he could do was wait. His thoughts raced: what about his team? What had become of the *Independence*? He needed to rest, to calm himself and to prepare.

Breathing deeply, Storm sat with his back against the metallic wall of his cell and closed his eyes. Forcing his thoughts to equalize, he imagined a small dot of light behind his eyelids. He pictured the spot of light growing and expanding, becoming warmer and brighter until it surrounded him, permeated him, healing and cleansing him. The skills he had learned in remote corners of the globe often helped him in his fight, and the meditational techniques soothed him....

He had been meditating for some time before sounds outside his cell brought him back to reality. Sometime during his self-imposed trance, the light bulb had brightened to illuminate his tiny cell and the sense of motion had stopped. The vessel had arrived at its destination. Storm's head was clear and his thoughts untarnished, and he was ready when the hidden door to his cell opened. A smoothly pivoting steel section that had fit incredibly flush with the rest of the wall before him now swung outward and the silhouettes of men appeared in the hall outside.

Storm launched himself at them, crashing into the first of the men with his shoulder. He let momentum carry him to the ground and he twisted as he fell, landing on his back. Another one of his captors barely had time to turn around to face him before Storm's booted feet lashed out from his position on the floor and kicked him in the face, sending him into the wall and to the ground.

Kicking his shackled legs out again and contracting his body, Storm launched himself from where he lay supine on the floor into a standing position. Another captor was stepping forward to try to wrestle him down; Storm clenched his hands together and swung them, the double fist colliding with the side of the man's head. As his target stumbled Storm brought his arms over and down around his head, wrapping the short chain between his wrist shackles across the man's throat. He pulled back and drew the thug up in front of him as the helpless man fought against the chain that was strangling him.

A click at Storm's left temple caused him to freeze. The cold muzzle of a pistol pressed into his flesh there. "I've heard all sorts of things about you," a voice said, "but none of 'em used the word 'bulletproof.' Let 'im go, hero. You ain't goin' anywhere."

Storm released his captive, who promptly spun around and slugged the adventurer in the gut. Storm doubled over, coughing as little lights swam in his vision. As he caught his breath he heard the one with the gun tell the other, "Don't do that again! He's supposed to be in one piece when we deliver him."

"Yeah, and right now I still count just one piece of this jerk," the other retorted. He refrained from attacking Storm again, however.

"All right," the pistol-wielding tough addressed Storm again. You're gonna march ahead of me now, and don't think I won't drill you in the back of the head. If you're gonna live you're supposed to be untouched but you don't gotta be alive. Orders say if you try and make a break for it we gotta do what we gotta do, *comprende*?"

Storm nodded, looking each of the men in the eye. The one who gut punched him grinned like a shark.

"Okay, then start walkin'," he was told.

After they removed the shackles from his ankles so he could walk easier, Storm was led by the four men down a long series of cramped hallways. He tried to get an impression of the craft he was aboard but any time he slowed down the gunman would jab his pistol into Storm's ribs. Finally, the trip ended with an open door and the dim interior of the craft was flooded with light from outside.

The pirate in front of Storm hopped down onto the rocky ground below the open hatch and Storm looked around. They were in a massive cave, with a soaring roof that extended up past the bright lamps that were hung there and illuminating the cavern. It was impossible to tell exactly how big the space was, as parts of it extended off into darkness beyond the lights, but it was large enough that a few trucks were seen to be driving along paths with supplies and crews. Small structures, workshops and shacks of some kind littered the open and flat expanse of rocky ground before him.

"C'mon, get goin'," the pistol-toting thug growled behind him.

During his struggle, Storm had been careful not to crush or damage the glass vial he had hidden in his hands. With the slightest of motions, he now dropped the small vial to the ground and hopped down onto the rocky cave floor, his right boot heel crushing the glass container. Storm inconspicuously ground his heel into the glass, both to further pulverize the pieces of glass and to ensure that the vial's contents was smeared over as much of the bottom of his boot as possible. Glancing at his captors, Storm was assured that none of them saw his actions. He marched ahead, mentally crossing his fingers.

After walking ahead for a few more moments, Storm allowed himself a quick peek at the craft they'd just left, and he couldn't help but be impressed. The craft had been a submarine, but not of any kind of design that he'd ever seen before. The long steel tube was slightly flattened, its conning tower low and almost non-existent. Studded around the top of the craft were several hydraulic arms of some kind, though these were folded and not in use at the moment. At the rear of the submarine a crew was maintaining some kind of equipment, but Storm was unable to get any further impressions as the gunman poked him again.

"Keep movin' an' don't worry about sightseein'," he said, "I'm sure there'll be plenty of time for that later." One of his companions barked a single, harsh laugh.

Storm complied and continued onward, following their lead as he was herded through tunnel after winding tunnel. Along the way, they passed many other people: some of them were normal, and these rough men stopped and stared as they recognized the face of the renowned adventurer and jack-of-all-trades that had been captured. Others seemed blank and robotic, staring straight ahead and paying no attention to anyone as they went about their business.

One of these, Storm recognized as one of the group of would-be saboteurs and murderers from F.P. 1. One of his warders called out to the lanky gangster.

"Hey, Jimmy, look who we nabbed!"

The tall zombie-like man just kept walking and didn't answer to the calling of his name. The one who called out to him shook his head sadly and kept walking. After failing Poseidon, Jimmy just wasn't himself anymore, and was just like the other automaton-like worker drones.

The tunnels the group traversed seemed endless and maze-like, and Storm was doing his best to remember the way out just in case he was able to escape, but it was becoming harder and harder to keep track of all the twists and turns. Just as he began to wonder exactly how much farther he was going to be led, the group arrived at the stone steps and the guarded iron door of Poseidon's chamber.

The guards on either side of the door nodded at the password that was given, and they swung the door swung open for the group to admit their hostage into the throne room.

CHAPTER 17: FACE TO FACE WITH THE SEA GOD

"**I** knew it was you, Manton," Storm said to the tall, dark clad personage that stared down at him from the throne.

Roderick Manton raised a single eyebrow as he stroked his black mustache. He seemed amused. "Oh? Do tell."

Storm ignored him and looked around the dome ceilinged chamber. "Swell place you got here, nice and dank. Let me ask you a question: what kind of bat problems do you have in here?" He looked around and his mocking fell silent; Poseidon/Manton wasn't alone: the four thugs who had escorted Storm from the submarine had followed him into the throne room, but Manton had been flanked by three more men who had been standing in the shadows. Storm could see them more plainly now and he recognized two of them as saboteurs from F.P. 1: these were the hulking Packer (whose arm was out of the sling but still bandaged) and the weaselish Oakley, who beamed with pride at his capture of the troubleshooter. The third man was one that Storm had both hoped and dreaded to see here; it was Herbert Chalmers. The former MARDL scientist stared blankly at Storm and showed no emotion or recognition at all.

"I see you've met some of my associates before," Manton said. "They failed to get you on Flying Platform 1, but they've redeemed themselves by bringing you here before me today."

"Herbert," Storm addressed his friend and former employee. The scientist's face never twitched.

"Yes, I believe you know Mr. Chalmers here as well. He's part of my organization now, whether he likes it or not."

"What do you mean?"

Manton waved away the question. "All will be revealed in time." Then to his men: "Remove his shackles, and then you're free to leave. Oakley, Chalmers, please keep our guest covered."

The gangster drew a pistol and pointed it at Storm, and Chalmers robotically followed suit. Something was very wrong with the normally gentle scientist.

The group who had led Storm from the submarine removed the bonds from his wrists, and then quietly exited the throne room, the iron door clanging shut behind them.

"Now, Mr. Storm, how did you know I was behind 'Poseidon's curse?'"

"It wasn't too hard to figure out," Storm explained. "You were on the first ship to disappear, and after I noticed that the second ship that disappeared belonged to Steven Reagan, and that he was aboard it, I thought it was too coincidental that the same fate should befall two men who had previously dealt with one another. Of course it could have been started by someone before you, someone who had indeed stolen you and your crew as their first victims, but I figured if there was an insider on board one of the ships it would have been you." He smiled crookedly. "I'm not the world's greatest detective; I'm just the first guy to make the connection. Now what's it all about?"

Manton stood up from his gilded throne. He picked up the Greek theatrical mask of Poseidon where it lay next to his seat and examined it. "'What's it all about?'" he said, repeating Storm's query. "In a word? Power."

Storm was silent as Manton went on. "In the old days of this part of the Earth, men would tremble at the thought of the power that their gods held over them and over the world around them. They paid tribute to the gods regularly, through offerings and sacrifice intended to keep their gods from being angry with them. It was all about respect for the power that they held over mortals, and the fear of what the gods would do to them if they were not appeased." Manton looked from the mask to Storm. "Imagine that kind of feeling, Mr. Storm. Imagine what it would be like to be a god, to make people quake in fear. Imagine what you could accomplish with that kind of power and respect."

"I can't," Storm replied, "I don't *want* to imagine that feeling. For a mere man to have that kind of power; that's not respect, that's a dictatorship."

Manton laughed. "A dictatorship? No, it's far better than that; it's a feeling *higher* than that." He set down the mask of Poseidon again. "Fate has brought me the means of wielding that kind of power, Storm. It's my destiny. In my days as an explorer, I was a conqueror of the natural world. If given the means, why wouldn't I choose to conquer the world of men as well?"

Storm was silent, gauging the man. Did he really believe he was fated to hold sway over mankind? Was it just rhetoric, or his actual goals, or was he insane?

Manton sighed. "I suppose I'd best start at the beginning, so you can understand my intentions and the tools which I will use to gain them." He turned and began walking to the rear of his chamber, to one of his tables in the back. "Follow me, Mr. Storm. As long as you don't make any sudden moves, Mr. Oakley and Mr. Chalmers will feel no need to perforate you."

Storm climbed the steps to the throne platform and followed Manton to his table, followed closely by the eyes and guns of Oakley and Chalmers. As he passed under it, Storm glanced upward at the skylight at the top of the domed ceiling. He noted to himself that it was night outside and he wondered what had become of his friends and crew. He also recalled Poseidon's threat to attack Limenas Thasou and wondered if it had been a ruse all along to lure the MARDL ship into a trap.

Manton was pointing to a photograph on the table, which was carefully arranged with all manner of documents and bric-a-brac. "This photograph is the last picture taken of me before I found my power," he said to Storm, "Before I became Poseidon."

The photo was of Manton and his team of explorers and scientists, including Chalmers. The group was standing around and smiling at the stern of a ship. Painted on the hull beneath them was the ship's name: the *Dryad*. They all seemed happy and friendly with each other, a group that seemed to be getting along. *How did things change to get so far from that?* Storm wondered.

"On that day, my team and I made a dive to investigate the sediment on the seabed. We were west of the Cyclades, in dangerously deep water." He turned to Storm: "Are you familiar with Joseph Salim Peress and his creation, the Tritonia atmospheric diving suit?"

Storm nodded. He knew of the British engineer and his creation: a uniquely armored and fortified suit of mechanically enhanced "armor" that would help protect divers in extreme depth or adverse diving conditions.

Manton continued. "Well, we had a pair of his wonderful creations aboard and an associate and I used them to dive to the sea bottom. It's truly an amazing feeling down there, Storm. It's as if you're on the surface of another world. Time and light and motion all seem to have different meanings for you when you're deep down at the bottom of the sea." Manton's eyes sparkled for a moment with a distant light as he reminisced, then he blinked and continued.

"We weren't looking for anything special there, mind you, we just wanted to examine the sea floor and take samples of the silt. Once we arrived at the bottom we were very shocked to discover something none of us expected: a pair of human skeletons almost right at our feet. They were remarkably preserved somehow, petrified and fused to the stones around them, but they were unmistakably human. After examination we found that one was male and the other female, and believe it or not they were still clutching hands; a final act of love in the midst of their death. It was quite moving, but it was also the heralding of something even more incredible.

"My team and I continued to dive that day, uncovering more and more evidence of a city nearby," Manton continued. "It was all rubble, of course, marble and stone blasted and crumbled and knocked about by either age or a cataclysm of some kind, but it was a city nonetheless. It would probably have been a major archaeological find to the rest of the world, perhaps even being the source of Plato's tales of lost Atlantis. All we had to do was report it and we'd all be famous men of science."

He paused as he picked up another photograph. "Fate," he began again, "would have a very different plan for me, however." He handed Storm the picture.

The photograph was a little blurry and hard to make out, but Storm could discern some kind of irregularly shaped rock in the foreground. At the bottom of the photo, someone held a measuring tape across the boulder: the rock measured a little under five and a half feet in diameter. Behind the rock, a face could be glimpsed: it was looking off to the side, and the look in the face's eyes was full of worry and fear. The unknown man was clearly disturbed by something.

"This rock," Manton explained, "sat near the heart of the sunken city. It was all by itself, unmolested by any kind of decay or buildup of sediment. It gave off its own light; a very strange find. We knew we had to bring it to the surface, and on the next dive we harnessed the rock and had it pulled up onto the Dryad's deck."

Manton took the picture from Storm's hands. He looked at it, almost in reverence of his bizarre find. "As we set about examining the stone meteor, whatever it was, it became apparent that there was something special about it. Anyone who came into contact with the stone felt strange. They described the feeling as 'drained' and 'trance-like' and the feeling increased the longer they touched the stone but dissipated when they were pulled away from it. I tried to feel it myself, but found that when I touched it I felt none of the things the others had experienced. At first, I was disappointed." He chuckled to himself before he continued, and Storm once again began to question Manton's sanity.

"The crew began to shun the rock, feeling it was cursed or even evil. I myself began to wonder about the rock's nature and considered dumping it back overboard. At the end of the day I lay awake and thought all through the night about the rock. I couldn't get it out of my head. The others feared it because of what it did to them, but it did *nothing* to me. It was a sign; it was a power that I alone could control.

"And so I started to use it on my crew, those small-minded people who would rather see it thrown back into the sea." Manton fixed Storm with a thousand yard stare, eyes hollow and eerie. "Chalmers," he called to the nebbish scientist without taking his eyes from Storm's. "Come over here, please."

Robotically, Herbert Chalmers approached his master, still holding his pistol on Storm.

"Show Mr. Storm your leash, Mr. Chalmers," Manton commanded.

As Storm watched, Chalmers pulled away his shirt collar with his free hand. There, tight around his throat, was a simple steel chain and in the center of Chalmers' throat was a small, roughly cut rock. It glowed ominously with a dim green light.

"My God," Storm breathed.

"Not yet, but I will be soon." Manton winked at Storm, who saw no humor in the maniacal declaration.

CHAPTER 18:
THE WEAPONS OF A
MADMAN

Without changing expression, Chalmers closed the collar of his shirt. Storm felt sick. What was going on in Chalmers' head, under the spell of that strange pendant? He had little time to consider this, because Manton's boasting had begun again.

"With the crew and my team of scientists under my control and obedient to my every command, I now had the power to begin making things happen," Manton continued. "It was all falling into place: I was becoming Poseidon, ruler of the seas. If you've studied your mythology, you may be aware that aside from being the Sea God, Poseidon was also believed to have caused mental disturbances, such as epilepsy and so forth. With this stone in my possession I had been given that ability, the key to the minds of men. And now, with the aid of my seismic and oceanographic specialists I set out to give myself the other powers attributed to Poseidon. Follow me."

Manton led Storm out of his sanctum and down the tunnels into the lowest reaches of his cavernous base. Along the way, Storm glanced at the other servants of Manton's that they passed. Some of them were robotic and glassy-eyed slaves of Poseidon's power, while others were obviously individuals who were going along with Manton of their own free will. Many sneered at Storm as he passed; the troubleshooter had made lots of enemies in his war on the predators of society, and they were all too glad to see him here and in the clutches of their master.

As they walked, Manton resumed his story. "I returned to the United States, but only briefly. I knew I would need willing men to help me undertake my conquest, and my old acquaintance Steven Reagan had access to criminals looking for reform. I knew that the promise of payment and plunder on a scale they'd never seen could help bring them back to their old ways, and so I made my plans. First, I visited Reagan and 'leashed' him with one of the pendants I'd fashioned from the rock

I'd found. Under my will, he was able to arrange for a construction ship to be loaded with former members of gangland who would find interest in my scheme, along with materials and supplies. I had already found this hidden series of caverns and grottos on a previous trip through Greece, and it was a perfect place to bring my new army and the raw materials; the perfect place from which to begin my rule."

Exiting a tunnel, Manton proudly swept his arm out at the open cavern before them. Drenched in powerful overhead lights, Storm saw a vast graveyard of ships of different size, all in various states of being dismantled. Around them on the rocky ground of the surrounding cavern were tons of steel and other building materials, all meticulously arranged by Manton's forces.

"These are the ships I have stolen as Poseidon. Some were taken for their crew; others were taken for their cargos. All are being used as thoroughly as possible to build my tools."

Manton led the group on, through another tunnel that wound its way through the rock of the cavern. Storm found himself impressed in spite of Manton's madness and evil. The operation was massive, in a scope that was ever-widening. The more of Poseidon's methods, tools, and lair was revealed to him, the more formidable Storm found his enemy to be. At the end of the winding tunnel Storm was shown a more fortified area: steel-reinforced walls lined this docking-bay and Storm realized they had come back around to a different area of the original cavern in which the sub that had brought him here rested. From this angle, he could see the strange submarine in all its glory. Next to it, tethered to another dock, was a second craft of the same design, though bigger and with more of the strange equipment the other sub had mounted near its stern. This submarine also had none of the strange hydraulic equipment that the top of the other craft had. In a separate area of the massive cavern, a dry dock had been constructed and here, nearly completed, was a third submarine that almost dwarfed the other two.

"These are the ships of my fleet. The smaller submarine is the one that brought you here: the *Athena*. She was built primarily for the capture of the other ships and for the boarding and combat of others who would oppose me and my will."

"Since you're showing off all your secrets, how about you fill me in on exactly how you accomplished those boat-nappings?" Storm said; his curiosity mixed with revulsion.

"Very easily," Manton replied. "When a ship is found that would prove useful to me and my empire, the *Athena* cruises near the surface and approaches the targeted ship. Once near, a smoke-screen device is extended above the waves in order to obscure visibility with a fog or mist. Once the *Athena* is beneath the ship, a chemical compound of my own creation…"

"You mean, 'of your slaves' creation,' of course." Storm chided.

Manton's anger flared momentarily but it dissipated. "A chemical compound *designed under my supervision* and thoroughly aerated with carbon dioxide bubbles is released beneath the target's hull. The compound rises to the surface of the water around the hull and when it comes into contact with the open air on the surface, it hardens into a thick, plastic-like substance that thoroughly encases the ship."

"The phony iceberg shapes in the water around my ship, and the small block that was carrying a body that was found several days ago…"

"Indeed!" Manton cut Storm off. "With this substance surrounding the ship and its propellers, it won't be going anywhere on its own. After ensnaring the ship in the 'ice,' my forces are launched aboard the targeted ship to ensure that the crew is going to be submissive, while those hydraulic arms on the top of the *Athena* are extended to clamp around the target and its encasing prison and hold it while being transported back to my lair. The boarding parties are outfitted in a suit of armor that is a heavily advanced form of Peress' Tritonia atmospheric diving suits: not only does it protect my men from the resistance of the targets' crews, but it uses various high pressure water systems as offensive weapons and as propulsion. Plus, the sight of being overrun by black suited armored 'sea monsters' is a bit unnerving, as I'm sure you can attest?" Manton smiled at Storm mockingly.

"They're not so tough, Manton. I'm sure you've noticed by now your crew has become a little smaller since my team and I became involved," he replied.

"Of course," the man who called himself Poseidon responded. "You are… *were* a most worthy opponent."

"I'm still in the running, Manton. Now, how about those freak waves? What are you doing to pull those off, 'sea god?'"

Manton grinned, and Storm couldn't help but smile himself at the man's megalomania. He was enjoying showing off his creations and methods to the adventurer. "Come, I'll show you."

Manton led Storm, along with Oakley and Chalmers, along an elevated steel walkway that overlooked the second submarine.

"The second, larger ship here is the *Proteus*, and it was constructed to carry out the testing and usage of a device my scientists devised under my direction. I call it the Seismic Hammer. The third ship, currently under construction, is to be the *Orion*. It will be able to carry my Seismic Hammers to anywhere, any target in the world. Soon, my rule will extend beyond the Aegean Sea. Greece is just the beginning, Storm. Soon my reach will cover all the globe. All the oceans and seas will be mine, and just like Greece the governments of the world will have to pay me tribute or see their coastal cities wiped from the map."

Storm realized that Manton's aim was much higher than any of them thought. He was planning on holding the world hostage by using the oceans against it. "So what are these Seismic Hammers, Manton?" Storm pried. The scope of Manton's world shaking mania was coming into focus, and here was the core of his power.

"As you know, many of the scientists aboard the *Dryad* were already in the study of geophysics and specialized in underwater earthquakes and tremors and things of that nature," Manton told him. "These kinds of occurrences are the cause of large scale wave activity, and so they were well versed in what kind of results that different kinds of tremors produce. I worked closely with those seismologists and my engineers to create a weapon, a device which I could attach to the ocean floor and produce intense, controllable vibrations. Using these delicately calibrated machines, I am able to produce waves of incredible size and force, and direct them at any target I wish. I used them to wipe out Katsopolis, which was the last target in the testing phase of the project. Earlier today I used them to attack Limenas Thasou and I even used one today to wreck your ship, the *Independence*." Manton grinned with triumph.

Storm flew into a rage. Though Manton stood nearly a foot taller than the adventurer, Storm took him by surprise by leaping up and head butting him in the center of his face. Storm's forehead collided with Manton's nose with a bone snapping crunch and blood burst out across the madman's face.

Immediately after landing back on his feet Storm kicked out his legs, striking the gun from Chalmers' hand with one kick then immediately sweeping Oakley's legs out from under him with another. Storm dove for one of the fallen pistols. Snatching it up, he rolled to his feet and brandished it, but as soon as his fight had begun it ended: a flood of Poseidon's forces

Storm's forehead collided with Manton's nose...

had seemed to appear out of nowhere and swarmed him. Storm was able to fire several shots and three of Manton's men fell before the gun was wrestled from his grip and he was slammed to the ground. He was pinned there, helpless in the face of so many combatants.

"You're no superman," Poseidon told him, his face streaked with his own blood though he appeared to not even notice. "You dare to think you can oppose me, a god on Earth?" He glared down at Storm, and then said to his soldiers. "The time has come, men, for Challenger Storm to join me and my rule. Bring him."

As Manton led the way, his men lifted Storm bodily from the floor. They applied shackles back to his wrists and his ankles again. Storm was a capable fighter, skilled in several different martial arts and combat disciplines, but the sheer number of Poseidon's swarm of men kept him from using those skills. He was without weapons and his tools now as well. Storm found himself completely overpowered.

Back through the tunnels the group moved, until at last they came upon a heavily barred iron door. This door was opened by Roderick Manton and the group of his soldiers followed him into the space that was revealed. Those who had joined Manton's cause of their own free will hated and shunned this place, and they were uneasy within its walls.

In the center of the small chamber, sitting on a raised platform, was the glowing green rock from the depths of creation. It had slammed into Earth thousands of years before, destroying a utopian island in the middle of the Aegean Sea. The strangely malignant rock had then waited beneath the waves for countless lifetimes before Roderick Manton had stumbled upon it. The fearful energy it radiated was palpable within this room to everyone but the man who styled himself Poseidon, ruler of the sea.

Clifton Storm himself felt strangely light-headed within the room, and he struggled again now, more fiercely than ever, against those who held him. Manton went to work on the rock, using a hammer and chisel to carve a small, irregular chunk from the leprous green stone. Attaching it to a small steel chain, he turned toward Storm and approached him with reverence, as though he were carrying out some kind of deadly ritual. Without a word, Manton placed the tight chain around Storm's throat, the green stone flush against the helpless troubleshooter's flesh.

The men who served Poseidon set down Storm and stood back, aware of what would happen next.

Suddenly free, Storm moved to try to snatch the chain from his neck, but his limbs were slow to respond. He felt like jelly, and a strange buzzing was filling his head. The buzzing sensation rushed into his brain like water filling a bottle. He writhed pitifully upon the floor, his mind struggling against the invasion within his head. Storm felt thought leaving him, his memories becoming vague and detached. He was watching his free will race away, a train passing him and leaving down a dark tunnel. His last conscious thoughts were wracked with guilt. He had let everyone down: his team, himself, those who would suffer at the hands of a madman, the world. He had failed.

It was over. Storm lay there on the floor of the chamber in a fetal position, panting and glassy-eyed. His eyes saw everything, but nothing within his mind connected his thoughts with what he saw.

"Get up, on your knees," Manton commanded him. Storm did as he was told, his mind doing only as it was instructed and nothing else.

"From now on, your allegiance is only with me, Clifton Storm. Tell me now: who do you serve?"

"I serve only Poseidon," Storm said, his voice flat and disconnected. Manton grinned back in evil triumph.

CHAPTER 19: ADRIFT BUT NOT YET BEATEN

The *Independence* was still without power and communications, and it drifted on the night waves. While the medical staff tended to the wounded, crews were still hard at work repairing the numerous damages to the ship and its functions. The repairs were slow going because of the lack of electrical power, and they were doing their best to tend to everything by flashlight. They had been unable to launch any search parties yet. The launch bay was still out of commission: the massive doors were unable to be opened yet, and many of the planes and boats within had sustained heavy damages. The breaches in the hull were being patched up; and they were lucky that the watertight seals between sections had proved effective enough to keep the ship from flooding too much. Meanwhile on the deck, crews were doing their best to prepare for the return of electricity. Once power was returned to the craft they would be utilizing the cargo and utility cranes to try to hoist the radio tower back into place. The repairs were being worked around the clock, and though most of the crew was tired and ragged by now, they kept up the pace and did their best to repair the damages speedily.

Somewhere out there, Poseidon was winning. He had no doubt carried out his attack on Limenas Thasou by now and who knew what he was planning or threatening next? He also had their beloved leader in his clutches, and there wasn't a person on board the *Independence* who wasn't worried about Clifton Storm. They knew he would want them to carry on, to continue onward and do their best to find and stop Poseidon, and they did their best to fix their broken vessel so that they could do just that. They hoped for the best, but they all had their fears for the worst.

Diana St. Clair had been assisting the crew working within the beaten launch bay. She was exhausted, covered in grease and worn looking, a far cry from the almost glamorous adventuring aviatrix that had touched down in Miami days before and had sent Storm off in search of Poseidon's curse and Herbert Chalmers. Diana was tough as nails and had proven herself a fierce and deadly combatant, but here she was beginning to falter and weaken in the face of the *Independence*'s defeat. Gibb had gently but insistently sent her away from the launch bay repairs, urging her to get some rest and assuring her that there would be plenty of work for her to do when she returned. She laughed at his joke but appreciated the intentions behind it. She was tired and drained, and she knew she'd have to get some rest soon or risk burning out completely.

On her way back to her cabin, she passed by Storm's quarters and frowned in melancholy. She wondered where he was, if he was still alive and what he may be doing. As her eyes fell to the floor, she noticed a crack of faint light beneath his door. Someone was inside.

Quietly, she eased the door open to find Willy Avis within Storm's cabin. He was sitting behind Storm's cluttered desk, and in the light of a candle on the desk she could see him resting his elbow on the desk, his eyes covered by his hand.

"You okay, Willy?" she asked quietly.

The startled mechanic sat up, his sad eyes regarding her for a moment before dropping to the floor. "Yeah, I'm hanging in there. How about you?"

"I'm exhausted," she replied, sinking into one of the chairs in front of the desk. "Nobody can even begin to guess when we'll be able to get the launch bay doors open again, and in the meantime all the planes and boats are in a competition to see which of them is in worse shape." She smiled weakly for a moment, and he shared it. Then her smile fell.

"This is bad, isn't it?"

Willy nodded. "You bet it is. We've never been so sunk." He considered his choice of works. "Well, we're not actually *sunk*, thank God," he smiled, "but we're stuck and by that, I guess I do mean it literally."

The pair were quiet a moment.

"What if Cliff's... gone, Willy? I mean, really gone?" Diana finally asked.

Willy took a deep breath before answering. "We'll keep on. You know he'd want us to continue what he started. We'd just keep going and we'd make Poseidon pay along the way." His eyes hardened.

Diana sighed and rubbed her eyes. "I just wish we could get these repairs out of the way so we could get out there and look for him."

There was a muted thump somewhere in the ship and light suddenly flooded the cabin and the ship, along with a sudden and constant low humming noise. Power had been restored to the *Independence*.

"Well, that should help us a lot," Willy said. Diana's eyes sparkled, her fatigue suddenly forgotten.

The next two days passed in a blur for Clifton Storm. Under the influence of the strange stone's effects, he had no sense of time and robotically performed the tasks given to him by Roderick Manton.

Once he had Storm under his command Manton had immediately ordered him to work with him and his engineer slaves in designing a propulsion system for the super submarine, the *Orion*. With Storm's knowledge and creative ability added to the group, they wasted no time in devising a modified form of the same amazing engine that powered the MARDL ship, the *Independence*. Once the designs were finalized and the materials assessed, Poseidon's workers, both independent and "leashed" slaves, began working on the construction and implementation of the new engines.

After completing his work on the engines, Storm was assigned by Manton to begin working on a more efficient model of the Seismic Hammers. The pod-like devices, when dropped from Poseidon's submarines onto the seabed, were already deadly and amazing weapons and could only be made more so with Storm's intellect added to the mix.

Biological functions were regulated with robot-like precision. As one of Poseidon's mindless slaves, Storm had little need of sleep and just like the others he slept only when ordered to, and even then only kept asleep for a couple of hours at a time. Restroom visits were rigidly scheduled, as was eating and drinking.

Storm had been reduced, for all intents and purposes, to a machine: an intelligent, soulless machine that possessed all of his knowledge and skills but none of his thought or emotions.

The same two days passed agonizingly slow for the MARDL crew. Once power was restored, the repair work was able to be completed much easier, but the sheer amount of it was still overwhelming. Many of the crew felt no nearer to being able to continue the hunt for Storm, Chalmers, and Poseidon.

While the crew of the *Independence* struggled to get their feet under them again, a packet containing Poseidon's explicit instructions for ransom payments had arrived at the Greek House of Parliament at the Old Palace in Athens. Because of the wave that had indeed struck the island of Thasos, Grecian Prime Minister Alexandros Zaimis and the other members of Parliament were forced to take Poseidon's wild threat very seriously. The population of Limenas Thasou has been spared only because the town had successfully been evacuated, and they had watched in horror as wave after wave had assaulted and destroyed their little island city. The threat of Poseidon's attacks was all too real, and for the leaders of the country it became another log in the fire in which Greece found itself burning. The government grudgingly began to make arrangements for their first payment to Poseidon.

The money wasn't really the most important thing to Manton. The thing he cherished most about his newfound position was the fear it generated. Greece and the rest of the area were nearly trembling now, and soon the rest of the world would fear his might. The feeling of absolute power intoxicated him. When not working on the betterment of his designs for world conquest, Manton would spend hours alone in the chamber with the glowing meteor, his eyes entranced by the softly pulsing corpse light of the mysterious rock. It had come to him, empowering him by not affecting him with its strange energy. It almost seemed to whisper to him of the things he would have once he effectively ruled the world.

The repairs aboard the *Independence* were beginning to shape up at last. The radio tower had finally been hoisted back onto the deck and the ship once again had communications. When they were able to do so, the MARDL crew contacted the Hellenic Navy and asked for assistance. Storm and his team had originally attempted to keep their mission a secret in the Aegean, so as not to cause too much attention or trouble with the government who might have looked down upon an independent team of investigators snooping around in their waters. Now that Poseidon and his intentions had gone public, they had very little to lose. The frazzled Grecian government was only too happy to cooperate with the troubleshooters, who were slowly becoming world famous. A destroyer was dispatched to help the crew of the *Independence* repair their ship and equipment and the naval craft's arrival was greeted with cheers from the tired members of MARDL.

The launch bay repairs were soon completed, and one of the small floatplanes that had escaped heavy damages was dispatched to begin looking for anything in the area that may indicate the whereabouts of Poseidon's lair. It flew around-the-clock; its pilots looked for anything at all that would indicate the existence of a base of operations for Poseidon.

The searches were fruitless: nothing was seen that would indicate any trace of the madman and his forces in the Aegean. The plane's repeated passes turned up nothing but endless stretches of blue. The plane, however, was small and had a limited fuel range. The longest-range aircraft at the adventurers' disposal was the *Longshot*, but repairs were still being done on the Consolidated Commodore that had delivered Storm and his companions to the *Independence*. The team waited, frustratingly, as work was being completed on the plane and on the rest of the ship.

They weren't beaten yet, but they were far from winning.

CHAPTER 20: GOOD THINGS IN SMALL PACKAGES

Diana St. Clair, Willy Avis, and Brock Thurman sat around a table in the *Independence*'s cafeteria. They had been able to get a little bit more rest now that they had assistance from the sailors from Greece, but they were still emotionally exhausted. They had finished their meal together in silence and sat brooding, alone with their thoughts and yet all sharing the same worry.

Diana finally broke the silence. "He could be anywhere."

The two men with her looked at each other and then at Diana.

"Poseidon, I mean, and Cliff and Herbert too, of course," she continued. "Who knows, they might be somewhere in the middle of the sea, they could be in Greece, Africa, Turkey, maybe they're not anywhere near us."

"Nothing is that fast," Brock put in. "They *have* to be somewhat close. Right, Willy?" he added hopefully.

Willy shook his head. "I've said it before, and I'll say it again," the aging mechanic replied. "We don't know what we're dealing with. Nothing about any of this seems right. I mean, Poseidon can control waves. We have no idea what else he's capable of."

The trio was silent again for a while. Finally, Diana spoke up again.

"Well, if anything happens to Cliff, I'm sure there would be enough people crying out for vengeance that Poseidon, whoever and wherever he is, won't be able to get too far in this world. He'll be a marked man."

They were silent again. Willy cocked his head.

"A marked man," he repeated. His eyes suddenly seemed to focus on something and he snapped his fingers and stood up. "Diana, I think you may have just found Cliff." He started to walk away from the table.

"Huh?" Brock and Diana said, looking at each other. They bolted up from the table and hurried after Willy, who had already left the cafeteria and was sprinting up a nearby stairwell.

"Willy, what's going on?" Diana called after him.

"A hunch," he called over his shoulder. "God, I hope I'm right."

Willy reached the door to Storm's quarters with Diana and Brock close behind him. He unlocked the door and they stepped in, and Willy immediately went to Storm's desk. He began to open drawers, searching for something.

"I swear, I don't know how he finds anything in all this mess," he muttered as he rifled through the papers. Then, to Diana and Brock, he explained: "About a day before we had the run-in with Poseidon's forces, Cliff told me he was working on something in the lab, a private project he'd been thinking of since we'd come out here onto the ship. He wanted to make sure that if one of us got swept overboard or otherwise lost, we'd be able to find them."

Willy shut the last drawer of the desk and moved to a nearby drafting table, which was just as cluttered and littered with paperwork as the desk was. "Originally, he wanted to make some kind of transceiver that would send out a distress signal when submerged in water. In the meantime, though, he also had an idea for a chemical compound that contained a unique low level radioactive isotope he'd discovered by accident: the Reese particle. The compound containing the isotope could be found by scanning it with a particle detector that had been worked up by the labs back in Miami. Ah-ha!" Willy yanked several sheets of paper, one of them a blueprint, from a stack of papers on the drafting table. The action resulted in an avalanche of papers and books that slid off the table and buried one of his feet, but Willy was oblivious to this and raced to an adjoining room in Storm's quarters, which was a small laboratory, one that was intentionally clutter free for safety reasons.

"I think Cliff may have been working on this project here because he brought this paperwork, and if I know him he may have started testing it on his own out here." He began to examine the list of ingredients in the chemical compound and comparing them against the contents of the lab's cabinets. "And I'm seeing a bit is missing from each of these components. We need to get to the ship's main labs right away." He turned and grinned at Brock and Diana. "The marked man that we need to be looking for right now isn't Poseidon, it's Cliff."

When Storm had broken the vial under his heel as he left the *Athena*, he had indeed been using the radiochemical marker he had been testing. He had actually strapped it to his leg earlier in the day before Poseidon had made his radio announcement and had been planning on testing the particle detector's range later on. Between Poseidon's threat broadcast, the race to Thasos, and the subsequent events of the ambush Storm had forgotten all about the experimental marker until he found himself without gadgets in the hold of the submarine. The reason behind his smashing the marker's vial was to ensure maximum spread of the chemicals upon his boot heel as well as the ground he walked on. He had regretted not telling more people, and had been hoping against hope that Willy Avis would remember his idea and start using it to look for him soon.

After he had been "leashed," Storm had ceased to hope or even think about rescue. In his obedient trance, he would have told Manton all about the marker if he had been asked about it. Luckily, the megalomaniac's ego prevented him from considering that Storm had any chance of escape and he never bothered inquiring about any such thing to Storm at all.

As Willy and the team aboard the *Independence* began looking into using this new angle in their search, Storm was trudging with other "leashed" slaves to the dining area inside Manton's lair. At the tables, they ate without a word while the talk among the independent lackeys of Poseidon at nearby tables was jubilant and loud. From the end of one table of mindless slaves, no one noticed the eyes of a small boy, as he glanced down the table at Storm. The boy's eyes brightened momentarily as he recognized the adventurer, then swiftly the boy retained composure and pretended to be zombified as he had been doing for some time.

Inside his head, the boy's mind was free. A plan was starting to take shape within him.

Later that night, the slaves' quarters were silent. A pair of guards played cards at a table nearby but had been lulled into complacency by the fact that no slave had ever fallen out of Manton's stone pendants and their strange effect on them. The guards never noticed the small and stealthy shape of the young boy as he crept from one room to another, seeking one slave in particular.

Creeping quietly up to the bunk in which Storm slept, the boy double checked to make sure. He was now positive that this was the man from the papers, the one they called "Challenger" Storm. He recognized the face, and the three telltale scars on the left side of the lean, handsome countenance. As quickly and as carefully as possible, the boy reached behind Storm's neck and undid the clasp on the pendant's chain. Once the chain was unlinked, he drew the chain and the stone off of Storm's throat.

With a gasp, Storm awoke with wide, shocked eyes. His fists were already swinging through the air, and the boy had been prepared for this: he had only a few people removed from the pendant's hold before and there was always a moment of struggle. He hurriedly put a hand on Storm's mouth.

"Shh!" the boy hissed, putting a finger against his lips. Storm fought the sudden tide of panic as his mind calibrated itself. He had memories of working on Manton's engines and on the design of the improved Seismic Hammers, had memories of doing everything he'd done for several days under the strange influence, but these were fleeting and dreamlike. His last real memory, at least the last one that felt real, was of fighting the strange effects of the stone pendant.

Storm reached to his neck and felt for the stone. The boy shook his head and held up the chain for Storm to see. Storm nodded and the boy removed his hand from his mouth. He crept to the doorway and peered around the corner at the guards as they played cards near the barrack's entrance. Storm had gotten up and was looking now, too, at the two armed men as they sat beneath the single bulb at the end of the hallway. They were engrossed in their game and didn't notice them.

The boy tapped Storm's arm and beckoned for him to follow him in the opposite direction, deeper into the slaves' quarters. The adventurer followed him and soon they came to a supply room. A table was in one corner where the rock ceiling was low. A table stood directly below an air duct, and the boy climbed onto it and reached up, removing the duct's vent cover. The boy climbed up into the vent, and Storm followed, putting the vent cover back in place when he was inside the duct.

Storm followed the boy as he crawled along the ductwork until they came at last to a junction of sorts. It was still cramped but large enough for them both to sit comfortably within the space. A little light filtered into the junction, and Storm could see the remains of some pilfered food containers.

"Obviously you've been using this space for some time," he said to the boy, who only smiled and shrugged.

"English? Do you speak it?" Storm asked the boy, who replied with something in Greek. Storm groaned and rubbed his forehead: he had been trying to learn languages since he started his war on criminals, and he had learned Spanish, German, Italian, Russian, Japanese, and several Chinese dialects. He still had a list of languages he'd yet to learn, though, and Greek was on that list. There were translators aboard the *Independence* that could speak it, of course, but he was stuck here without them.

"'Nikos,'" the boy said, tapping his chest. He repeated his own name, and then pointed at Storm. "Challenger Storm," he said.

Storm nodded. "Yeah, that's right, Nikos. Challenger Storm," he said. He was surprised that his work and his media given nickname, a nickname Storm himself wasn't entirely thrilled with, had been spread all this way from the United States. Storm tapped his own chest and said, "Call me Cliff."

Nikos nodded in agreement and repeated "Cliff," then said "Miami?"

Storm smiled. "Yeah, right: Miami." He pointed to himself, and then pointed at Nikos. "You?"

Nikos' eyes grew sad as he pointed to himself and said "Katsopolis."

Storm frowned sympathetically. "That's tough, kid... I'm sorry." They were both silent for a moment, then Storm cleared his throat. "Right. Well, now that we've been introduced, how is it that you're free?" Storm asked the boy. Nikos looked puzzled, and Storm mimed reaching for his neck to indicate the chain, and then pointed at the boy.

Understanding dawned on the boy's face, and he opened the collar of his shirt and showed Storm that he was still wearing his own slave pendant. Storm's puzzled face caused Nikos to explain by removing his pendant, then replaced it. Then he removed it again and placed Storm's pendant to his neck. Even with this other pendant around his throat he somehow retained his will and removed it.

It was Storm's turn to understand: Manton had been wrong. He *wasn't* the only person unaffected by the strange rock's influence. Apparently, a very small portion of humans were immune to the effects of the bizarre stone. Nikos had been kidnapped after Katsopolis had been struck by Manton's wave, but had somehow been able to hide his immunity to the stone pendant's effect in order to survive. That meant hard work and very little sleep while waiting to make a break for safety and freedom. It had to have been hard on the boy, who had probably lost everyone dear to him when Katsopolis was sacked by Manton.

"You're tough, kid, I'll give you that," he said to Nikos. Now we gotta do something to stop this guy." Manton was closing in on beginning his attacks against Greece, and as soon as the *Orion* was completed, he would be taking his attacks elsewhere in the world. Time would be even shorter for Storm and Nikos, too; he knew that soon it would be discovered that he was missing from the ranks of Manton's slaves, and the whole base would be swarming with those looking for them.

CHAPTER 21: THE HUNT FOR A MARKED MAN

It was nearing dawn, and the ghostly light on the horizon lent a dreamlike quality to the waves around the *Independence* and the Greek destroyer that had come to its aid, the *Syracusia*. Slowly, the massive doors of the *Independence*'s launch bay rolled open and exposed the flooded interior to the Aegean Sea outside. A few minutes later, the *Longshot* taxied her way out of the bay and away from the huge ship. After revving her engines up to speed, the wide-winged craft gracefully broke free from the deep blue water and climbed into the clear air. The plane banked and headed south, and its outline was different now than it had been before: a unique metallic frame, light weight but extremely strong, was attached to its tail. Nestled in this framework, a large, rounded metallic shape was cradled. When the craft was on the surface of the sea, the mysterious pod had been underwater and had been revealed only once the *Longshot* had lifted off, and the unique materials and construction of these additions did very little to weigh the plane down or change its aerodynamics.

Aboard the aircraft, Diana St. Clair smiled behind the controls. It felt good, exhilarating, really, to be finally in the air and on the search for Poseidon and his hostages. Beside Diana, Brock Thurman, and Willy Avis there were nine other crewmembers from aboard the MARDL ship: all of them were outfitted with binoculars with which they scanned the blue water beneath them.

In the center of the Commodore, a complicated machine had been bolted into place. Rising up from the floor, a pedestal had been secured upon which a box-like affair swiveled on a joint. At the end of this machine was a tube, and Brock held the box by the handles at the other end. Meanwhile, another series of machines and controls were set up and secured at the other side of the plane's converted passenger space. Seated behind this bank of indicators and monitors, Willy made adjustments to the sensor pedestal and its connecting arrays. When he was satisfied, he keyed his throat-microphone.

"Diana, we're all set here and ready to go. Just let us know when we're in position."

The comely woman in the pilot's seat responded. "We're nearly there, Willy. Give me about five minutes or so."

Shortly afterward, the *Longshot* found itself in position on the first point of its search grid just as the first rays of the sun began sparkling off the blue water below. Diana contacted Willy to let him know that they were ready, and she banked the plane and began heading west.

Willy gave a thumbs-up to the searchers aboard the *Longshot* and nodded to Brock, who flipped a switch on the box contraption. Instantly, one of the monitors on Willy's instrument bank lit up: a round convex screen decorated with a circular grid pattern. Willy donned a second set of headphones and intently watched the screen, making notes on a nearby pad and adjusting the mechanisms as Brock slowly turned the barrel of the particle detector's scanner.

Painstakingly, the *Longshot* flew over the Aegean Sea as the watchers and delicate sensors aboard swept the waves below it. The search had begun.

"Find them, you fools!"

Roderick Manton was in a rabid fury. A guard check among the leashed slaves turned up two missing members of Poseidon's workforce. Clifton Storm and Nikos were gone, and a rapid search for them had so far turned up no trace of their whereabouts.

Foam and spittle flew from Manton's lips as he screamed orders at his lackeys. The domed throne room rang with the echoes from his furious outbursts.

"I don't care who he is, he's just one man with a little boy! He can't have gotten far. I want him found! I don't know how he got loose and I don't care. I demand that he be brought before me!" Outrage burned intensely within him: here, Manton had held complete control over all within his reach; that control had suddenly been wrestled from him, toppled as he had slept by unknown means. Nobody had ever escaped from his influence in all the time he'd been building his empire and regardless of whether he wanted to admit it to himself, Clifton Storm had been the one person he thought might be able to defeat him. Storm's existence as a free and random element within his kingdom deeply troubled the man who called himself a sea god.

Oakley, Packer, and several other lieutenants of Poseidon bolted through the door of the throne room, relieved to be away from Manton's withering hate. They quickly organized their men into groups to spread out and search the hideout. As the squads of henchmen scrambled in their search, they were as yet unaware that two more of the unwilling workers had also turned up missing.

Storm and Nikos had successfully freed both Herbert Chalmers and Steven Reagan, who were among Manton's most prized servants. Before releasing them, Storm had successfully neutralized a pair of guards and left them tied up in storage lockers. He handed out the guards' weapons to the ex-MARDL scientist and the philanthropic industrialist and gave each of them a brief explanation on how to use the Tommy guns.

"I can't believe all of this," Reagan muttered as he looked around. The normally well attired businessman was grimy and dirty, and his eyes were wild. He had been among those who had been under Manton's spell for the longest: after he'd been forced to supply Poseidon with willing thugs, Reagan's nightmare of harsh labor had been long indeed. "How could he have done this? How could I have helped him?"

Storm put his hand on his shoulder, and Reagan focused on the adventurer's scarred face. "Mr. Reagan, I need you to focus on the task at hand for me. I know you remember part of the story; I'll fill in the other details for you later. Right now, though, I need you to help me. You and Nikos are going to free as many of the slaves as possible. There's strength in numbers here, and we're going to need as many of these kidnap victims as possible to free the others. Once everyone is turned loose, I want them all loaded onto one of Manton's subs. Use the *Athena*: it's the primary troop carrier and should hold the most personnel. Can you do that for me?"

Reagan gulped and nodded. He wasn't used to carrying weapons and being in combat situations, but the fact that he would soon have an army of others behind him bolstered his confidence. Storm's raw energy, set into decisive motion by the developing jailbreak, was contagious and Reagan felt that he could take charge of his part of the plan.

Storm turned to Chalmers. "Herbert, you and I are going to cripple Manton's Seismic Hammers. If he manages to get away, we need to make sure he won't cause any more of his freak waves." The nebbish scientist nodded and grinned; when he had been with MARDL, he had always been working in the home base and laboratories, never one to embark on adventures with Storm or his girlfriend, Diana St. Clair. Now that he was

"I can't believe this."

on the front lines, he was thrilled to see a little action.

After a final weapons-check, Storm hefted the automatic he had taken from a locker. "Okay, guys, this is it. Good luck to you all." He ruffled Nikos' hair and the boy smiled. "Reagan," he addressed the businessman, "Take good care of this kid. We owe him our freedom, and if we get out of this mess we'll owe him our lives." Reagan nodded soberly.

With that, the two duos parted ways and disappeared down separate tunnels.

The *Longshot* roared over the waves. They had been searching for almost two hours and so far nothing had turned up. The search team had not even considered giving up, though: there was roughly eighty-three thousand square miles covered by the Aegean Sea, and they wouldn't give up until every last one of those miles had been examined thoroughly. The watchers scanned the waves with their binoculars, ever hopeful of spotting something that would indicate the shred of a clue.

In the rear of the plane, Brock slowly turned the pivoting sensor of the particle detector. He began to wonder if the sensor and the intention behind its use were viable: even though Storm had been working on the isotope marker, it was debatable whether he actually had been carrying a prototype. Though he was as hopeful as the others, Brock also realized the possible futility of the search. It wasn't like looking for a needle in a haystack, but it was like looking for a needle in a haystack armed with a single tiny magnet. He stood straighter for a moment, stretching his back muscles and wiping the sweat from his brow.

In his headphones, Willy heard the tiniest "ping" sound. He threw his hand up and shot a glance over his shoulder at Brock. "Wait, wait... go back to where you had it." He watched the display screen, waiting to see if any visual indicator showed up.

Brock bit his lip; he had no idea where the sensor had been pointing when Willy had heard the noise, as it had shifted when he stretched. He aimed the detector in the rough area it had been as Willy lowered his hand. With the tiniest of motions, Brock swept the sensor's gaze through the direction again, wondering if Willy had imagined the sound after the miles and miles of silence they'd already scanned before.

Another ping in Willy's headphones, and he raised his hand again. Brock stopped moving the sensor immediately. The sound in Willy's headphones now remained constant, and at the furthest rim of the display's circular graph a faint green dot appeared. Willy checked a nearby compass and scribbled the heading on a pad, and then spoke into his microphone. "Diana, I think we got something, bearing East by Northeast."

Diana banked the plane, following the directions from Willy as Brock adjusted the sensor to keep it pointed in the direction of the blip. It remained on the display screen, rotating as the plane adjusted its course until it was directly at the exact top of the circle. The lookout in the cockpit couldn't see anything yet through his field glasses, but the blip on the screen in the back of the plane brightened slightly as they inched nearer to the source of the signal.

Tense minutes passed. As the signal slowly intensified, a tiny spot grew on the horizon in the lookout's binoculars: a dark spot on the seemingly endless expanse of dark blue below the aircraft. Soon the spot grew and details emerged. An island—really little more than jagged rocky formations—jutted up from the water. It looked uninhabited and uninhabitable, just a mass of stone sticking out of the sea.

In the back of the *Longshot*, Willy and Brock watched the spot as it grew closer and closer to the center of the display's graph, which indicated the plane itself. "We're almost on top of it," Willy said through the microphone.

"There's nothing down there but a bunch of rock, Willy," Diana said back through her microphone. "There's no buildings or any signs of life." The rocky island passed beneath the belly of the aircraft, and as it did, the signal disappeared from Willy's screen.

Brock swiveled the sensor around immediately, facing it now in the opposite direction it had been and pointing at the rear of the plane. The blip immediately returned to the indicator displays. "Well, that's gotta be it, Diana. The sensor isn't picking anything else up down there. Even if it's just a fluke reading, it's something. I think we'd better check it out."

Diana banked the *Longshot*, examining the rocky mounds again. Despite the fact that there weren't any visible structures on the island and no visible cave entrance at sea level, Willy was right, she realized: it *was* worth a shot and they had come prepared for a search both above and below the waves. "Okay, let me call it in and then we'll drop down and have a look."

Diana reported the coordinates of the island via radio to the *Independence* crew, who were in the process of finishing their repairs and were preparing to embark to wherever Storm was to be found. Finishing her radio transmission, she slowly dropped the Commodore down and gently landed the seaplane on the water. Her piloting skills prevented the aircraft from experiencing anything but a few minor bumps and turbulence as the big plane alighted on the waves. The watchers, in the meantime, had all focused their binoculars on the island in the distance: if Poseidon's base was indeed located there, there had been no activity to spot yet. It was entirely possible that they were also being watched by someone there on the island, hiding and waiting. Once the craft was settled and the engines killed, Diana joined Brock and Willy in their preparations at the rear of the airplane, while three of the crewmembers who had come with them readied weapons and gear.

Shortly afterward, the Commodore's engines started back up and it taxied before lifting off and headed back to the *Independence*, which was heading their way at that very moment. The outline of the craft was again different now than it had been upon arrival: the strange pod and framework affixed to the rear of the *Longshot* were altered, empty and folded up.

Beneath the waves, the small submersible from the *Independence*'s launch bay started its engines. The sub's hull was rounded, and a pair of portholes peered out over four folded manipulator arms at the craft's forward end. Painted on the side of the hull, a cartoon squid had been depicted in a fighting stance: four of the creature's tentacle were raised up and ended in boxing gloves, while its angry eyes scowled ahead in defiance. Next to the depiction was the nickname the sailors aboard the MARDL ship had given to the craft: *The Squintin' Squid*. Inside the sub, Willy, Brock, Diana, and the three armed crewmembers sat in tense silence as they headed toward the rocky island in the distance.

CHAPTER 22: THE CAPTIVES REVOLT

As Storm's friends made their way to the mysterious island, Steven Reagan and Nikos skulked through the cavernous hallway toward the slave quarters. The pair had already avoided two passing patrols of armed guards who were scouring the hideout looking for the escapees. Reagan was worried, and now was becoming doubtful: could they really hope to bring this whole operation down themselves? With the slaves freed from Poseidon's control they would have a better chance, but they had yet to do so. Challenger Storm was becoming known as a true force but his allies here weren't seasoned adventurers as he was, they were just a businessman, a scientist, and a little boy. Could they truly hope to turn the tide?

They rounded the corner and entered the workers' barracks. A single guard sat in the corner. As soon as he saw them he leaped to his feet, but as he reached for his weapon he was stilled when Reagan pointed his Tommy gun at him. "Don't do it," Reagan said to the guard, who in turn raised his hands above his head.

Reagan jerked his head toward the sleeping workers who were still in their bunks, and Nikos set upon his task of removing the chains from their necks. There was commotion as the leashed slaves were snapped from their control one by one. After the first few were released from their hold, Reagan commanded them: "Each of you start pulling those chains off the others, but don't touch the rock pendants themselves. When you free one, tell them to do the same for the others."

Reagan's head had been turned toward the slaves as he spoke, and he'd taken his eyes off the guard. Seeing his chance, the thug reached for his own gun. Reagan spotted the motion and he jerked, his trigger finger tightening reflexively as he fired a volley of bullets into the guard. The shots thundered and echoed through the room and the tunnel outside the barracks.

A nearby patrol in the tunnel stopped in their tracks as they heard the shots, then turned as one and bolted back to the source of the sound. The five man team rounded the corner and hurriedly approached the doorway to the barracks, readying their guns for what lay ahead.

A surging wall of humanity met them as they passed through the door, and although one of the guards managed to shoot down one of the rushing slaves the others were caught by surprise. The patrol was overwhelmed and beaten down by the suddenly freed unwilling workers of Poseidon. The revolt had begun.

Beyond the rocky walls of the mysterious and barren island jutting from the sea, the *Squintin' Squid* moved silently through the waves. Hidden beneath the surface, the tiny MARDL submarine was able to conduct its approach without being seen by potential watchers on the surface; within the craft, the small party was tense. The *Independence* was heading their way at full speed, the Greek destroyer *Syracusia* following at her heels. Both ships would provide aid if the barren spot turned out to be Poseidon's hiding spot, but until they arrived the troubleshooters would be on their own. They were well aware that they could be rapidly outnumbered, so stealth would have to be the most essential part of their raid.

Gradually, the group could see the stony walls of the island looming beyond the *Squintin' Squid*'s portholes. The pilot of the tiny craft, a skinny and freckled crewman named Scott, skillfully maneuvered the sub around the island's perimeter. Off the starboard side, Brock swept the craft's searchlight along the walls as he looked for something, anything that would indicate that this was more than just a random island somehow giving off the isotope readings. After about ten minutes, they found it.

The endless stony surface of the island's wall suddenly opened up into a large channel that extended back into the island's interior. From the surface, a collection of smaller stones sticking out of the water hid the channel, while a natural roof over it turned it into a tunnel and hid it from the air.

Cautiously, the crew guided the *Squid* into the tunnel. Risking a peek through the sub's periscope, Diana observed no watchers along the way, no hidden guards so far.

Arriving at the end of the tunnel, the group suddenly encountered an unexpected sight: a huge pair of metal doors. Searching carefully along the surface of the doors, nothing could be found to indicate a way to open them.

"Dead end," Scott said. "What do we do now, knock?"

"No, we go through it," Willy said. He had helped to design the submarine's equipment, and he took his place at the controls for the manipulator arms. These hydraulic appendages had been designed by

Storm and his think-tank as a means of aiding in salvage operations and the rescue of those trapped underwater. The arms unfolded from their resting place on the *Squid*'s forward hull, and Willy maneuvered them into position as he peered from the portholes of the craft.

Several minutes ticked by in tense silence. The arms moved along the surface of the doors, looking for a grip or a spot that the strong "fingers" at the ends of the arms could grasp to force the door open. There was no such spo;: the doors were tightly shut.

"I can't get them open," Willy finally said, deflated. "There's a cutting torch on one of the manipulators, I could try cutting it open."

"It's too risky here," Diana replied, staring thoughtfully at the doors. "Maybe we should look for another way in. This looks like Poseidon's front door, and I doubt it'll be that easy to get in this way. We still haven't combed the outside of this island, so there might be an alternative that we haven't found yet. I say we try to find another way inside first. If we can sneak in, it'll be all the better for us."

Brock nodded. "I agree. And if we can't sneak in the back door, we'll come back and through the front doors here, guns blazing and hoping for the best."

Folding the manipulators back up, Willy nodded in agreement. "Okay, Scott, take us out of here."

Storm and Herbert Chalmers had managed to get all the way down into Manton's most secure levels when the alarms started going off: a major riot was now taking place elsewhere within the complex, and the former slaves of Poseidon were revolting against their masters. Security had become lax in the area as Manton's troops were suddenly diverted from their searches for Storm and into crowd control efforts; the duo were now easily able to sneak into the laboratory and armory areas.

Stepping into the chamber which housed the Seismic Hammers, Storm and Chalmers confronted the lone pair of guards who had been left behind. The guards raised their guns, but the weapons of the escapees fired first and the soldiers of Poseidon collapsed limply under their bullets.

Chalmers was stunned; he had never taken a life before and stared glassy-eyed at the corpses. He was shaken out of his stupor as Storm snapped his fingers before his face. He focused on Storm's eyes.

"C'mon," the adventurer told him. "Stay with me, Herbert."

The scientist swallowed and nodded and he followed Storm to the Hammers. The pod machines were menacing somehow, even in their inactivity. At each one, the pair stopped and opened the waterproof access hatches. The wiring and sensitive gear work within was exposed to them this way, and they were able to make rapid changes to the machines. The wave-making devices would never be able to operate now.

Their sabotage completed, the pair moved on. In the next chamber, Storm found a group of leashed scientists, Chalmers' colleagues from the *Dryad,* toiling still at their work on the next generation of Seismic Hammers. These new models were intended to create even greater tremors and devastation on the ocean floor or even on the ground; Poseidon knew eventually he would have to extend his reach inland as well, and wanted optimum performance from the next wave of his deadly weapons.

Rapidly, Storm and Chalmers set to work removing the pendants from the mind-controlled scientists. After their initial spastic reactions the freed workers calmed down and were quickly filled-in on what was happening. Storm gave a pair of the scientists the Tommy guns taken from the slain guards. Bolstered by their freedom, the group was then led from the laboratory.

"Wait," a white bearded scientist suddenly cried out as he turned back. "There's a timed test I was conducting, I need to…"

Storm grabbed his arm. "No, there's no time for that. We've got to get everyone to the *Athena.* We're getting out of here."

As they entered the previous room, the scientist continued to protest. While Storm tried to reason with him, Chalmers turned and looked back a last time at the dead guards. His conscience itched within his brain, and the gentle scientist couldn't believe he'd had a hand in someone's death. Suddenly, Chalmers felt frozen in place: as he watched, one of the guards struggled where he lay wounded and raised a pistol toward Storm.

Chalmers gave a shout and leaped in front of the adventurer. A shot rang out from the guard's pistol and a red hole burst in Chalmers' torso.

Storm had spun when the scientist cried out; he drew aim with his .45 and fired, a single bullet striking the wounded guard in the center of his face. His head jerked back and dropped to the floor of the chamber, and the guard moved no more.

Chalmers staggered, his abdomen bleeding. He held his hands to the wound, then crumpled. Storm caught him and lowered him to the floor. One of the scientists took off his lab coat and handed it to Storm, who applied it to the wound and tried to stop the blood flow. It was difficult to tell the extent of the damage caused by the shot, and Storm did his best to treat the wound.

"No, no. Don't worry about me," Chalmers stammered. "I'm going to be okay. I don't think this heroic stuff is right for me." He smiled weakly and then grimaced in pain. "Cliff… you keep going, and knock the legs out from under Manton and his goons."

"You can't stay here…" Storm began.

"I know," Chalmers replied, struggling to his feet. Two of the scientists helped him up, propping him between them and draping his arms over their shoulders. "I'm going with these guys to the sub. You don't need me; I'm obviously a lousy shot, anyway." He smiled again.

Storm smiled and nodded back, and scooped up the Tommy gun Chalmers had been carrying. As the group of freed scientists reached the door, Chalmers turned to Storm.

"Oh, Cliff," he called back. "Don't forget about those damned armored suits. If Manton's goons strap into those there's no way any of us can put a dent in them without heavier weapons."

"Good thinking, Herb," Storm replied. "We'll make an adventurer out of you yet." He winked.

The group of former captives and their wounded friend left the room, and Storm stalked on through the complex, in search of the chamber of armor.

CHAPTER 23: CAVERNS OF DEATH

Stealthily, the man called "Challenger" moved through the corridors of Poseidon's compound. He had avoided a passing three-man patrol but had otherwise not seen any of Manton's goons as he made his way to the chamber where the suits of diving armor were housed. On his back was a rucksack that contained a large and heavy amount of explosives he had taken from the armory, and the weapons he had confiscated were fully-loaded now.

The tunnel through which he wound his way opened up and he was back at sea-level: across from where he stood, the enormous main cavern spread out before him. Across the water at the opposite side of the chamber Storm could see the former slaves of Poseidon boarding the *Athena*. A small crew of hostages had been taken by the rioting group: these hostages were crewmen of Poseidon's who were skilled submariners, and the rioters were forcing them to pilot the attack sub to freedom. There was a gunfight going on near the docks, and it looked as if Manton's soldiers were losing, outnumbered by the sheer volume of the freed captives. Storm smiled grimly. So far, things were going as he had planned. He only hoped for a minimum of casualties.

A sudden bubbling in the water nearby alerted him, and Storm drew back into an alcove, his weapon at the ready. He wasn't sure what was coming out of the water, but he wanted to be prepared.

He was not prepared, however, for the sight of the *Squintin' Squid* as it broke the surface of the dark water of the cavern.

After initially being unable to enter Poseidon's base through the main doors, the MARDL crew had left the tunnel and began a circuit of the rest of the rocky island's perimeter. They had begun to feel defeated when they came across a submerged vented hatch of some kind. It allowed water to flow freely into the compound and main chamber. The hatch had been too small and too far underwater to allow a ship to pass, but the tiny *Squintin' Squid* had been able to pass through it with no trouble at all once the manipulator arms had cut away the vented cover. After that, the sub had simply followed the utility tunnel into the main chamber. It was just dumb luck that the tunnel ended and the craft surfaced right near Storm's location.

The hatch of the tiny sub opened and Brock Thurman appeared with his machine gun at the ready. Storm emerged from the alcove and called to him, waving in relief.

"Well, geez, if I'd have known the cavalry was on its way I would have waited to start this party."

Spotting his friend and leader, the big man grinned and he climbed out of the sub and onto the nearby platform. Diana, Willy, and the other two crewmembers climbed out as well, leaving Scott inside at the controls for a getaway if needed.

Diana threw her arms around Storm and hugged him, as the others patted his back. Storm halted them. "Look gang: save it for later. There's a revolution going on here and everyone's going to need help getting out . There's the wounded to be taken care of, too." He turned to Diana. "And that includes Herbert: he's been shot, Diana. He was under Poseidon's control, a lot of us were, but we're free now. Look, it's a long story and I'll have to tell you later. In the meantime, I don't know where Herbert is, but he's being taken to that sub along with the others." He indicated the *Athena* at the other side of the cavern.

Diana's glad smile melted into worry: she had been elated to find Storm but her concern over her wounded partner took over now. She looked to the other side of the cavern and knew then that her heart still felt something for her old flame. The attraction that had been growing between her and Clifton Storm was only that: an attraction. She loved Chalmers, and she gravely feared for his life.

Storm picked up on her feelings, but he pushed his own away for the time being. "I'll explain everything later but right now we need help over there. We've got to get everyone out of this place. They're doing pretty good holding off Poseidon's men but they can't last forever on his home turf." He pointed up toward a room that topped a steel tower near the subs. "That's where the door controls are for this base. Open them up and blow the console. It's the only way to keep the doors open so everyone can get out. Brock, come with me." Storm and Brock turned away and began making their way back into the honeycombed tunnels of the cavernous base.

"Wait, where are you two going?" Willy called out to him.

"I need to take care of something, something that'll even up the odds a little bit."

As the two groups parted ways, Scott sat in the little submersible and watched them from the *Squintin' Squid*'s viewports.

"Hey… hey, what about me?" he called after them. "Guys?"

As his team took up the fight on the other side of the main cavern, Storm and Brock made their way through the tunnels until at last they came to the room where the suits of powered armor were kept. In the steel-walled chamber row upon row of the suits were kept in a state of constant readiness, their specially made batteries always charged and ready for combat. Storm would have liked to have get hands on one of the suits to learn its secrets, but there was no time for that now. He had to cripple the suits, had to stop Manton's men from using them.

Entering the room, Storm and Brock began to set the timed charges around the perimeter of the room and at the columns that supported the ceiling. The pair was engrossed in setting the explosives when suddenly gunshots rang out; the two adventurers ducked and sprinted for cover. A group of Poseidon's soldiers were entering the room from a doorway on the opposite side of the armor chamber. From his cover, Storm risked a peek at the soldier's positions. The chatter of gunfire burst out again and he ducked down, barely avoiding being struck by the bullets.

Storm and Brock looked at each other and the big bald strongman made a face. "This ain't good," he said and Storm gulped and nodded. The charges had been set with a short timer and they were nearing the point of detonation. The pair of men was pinned down behind a pillar, next to one of the very bombs that was ticking toward their explosive demise. They had to get out and very soon.

"Can you carry this thing while running?" Storm indicated a nearby empty suit of the powered armor.

"Probably," Brock nodded. "You know, one of these days you're gonna value me for more than just my strength," he chided as he reached up to remove the armor from its support.

"Well this ain't the day," Storm quipped as Brock nodded that he was ready. "Okay… go!"

The adventurer sprang from behind the pillar and fired a few quick bursts from his submachine gun, as Brock lifted the armor like a shield. Once Storm had the soldiers cowered for a moment he broke into a run for the other doorway, Brock running backwards behind him and holding the limp steel armor before him. Bullets bounced off the armor as the crew of Poseidon's soldiers began firing their weapons at the fleeing pair.

Just as Storm and Brock crossed the room's threshold, the explosive charges began to go off, drenching the chamber in thunderous fire. The concussion threw the adventurers to the ground outside in the tunnel, the empty armor laying across them heavily but protecting them from flying debris. With the supports and walls weakened the armor storage room collapsed in onto itself, burying the armor and the men within it as a dense cloud of dust kicked up and rolled along the tunnel.

Several seconds went by before Brock moved the limp armor aside. The two men sat up, coughing and covered in dust.

"Next time, maybe we set the timers for a little bit longer." Storm sighed.

"What's that?" Brock replied, wiggling his pinkie finger in his ear. "I can't hear you over that damned telephone ringing."

At the other side of the main cavern the freed workers of Poseidon were being ushered by Steven Reagan into the waiting *Athena*, while below the submarine's decks the captured crewmembers were being forced to make the engines ready for departure. Many of the captives had been experienced sailors and they were familiar enough with some of the operations aboard the ship, so that only a few of Manton's pirates were needed to sail the menacing submarine. The others were taken captive also, or killed during the uprising.

The opposing forces of Poseidon's men that were left had fallen back temporarily, and the shooting had lulled. Diana and the MARDL sailors had entered the tunnels to search for any stragglers or workers that were still under the bizarre effects of Poseidon's leashes, while Willy Avis made toward the control tower. At the top of the tower perched the small room that housed the controls for the lair's massive steel doors.

Just as he reached the tower's base, Willy looked up and was startled at the sight of Manton's brutish thug, Packer, as he entered the control room at the top of the ladder. Shots rang out from the control room, and a tight group of escaping workers was sprayed with bullets. They went down, bleeding from a dozen wounds.

Willy grimaced, and tossing the strap of his submachine gun over his shoulder he mounted the ladder. The wiry old mechanic climbed as fast as he could as bullets continued to rain down on the escaping captives. Over the sounds of shooting and the targets' attempts at defense, Willy could hear the rumbling and harsh chuckling: the thug was actually enjoying the bloodshed he was causing among the escapees. Furrowing his brow, Willy clambered up the final rungs of the ladder.

Packer stood in the corner of the control room with his back to Willy, a massive machine gun in his hands. It hammered as he fired another volley down on the groups below. The machine gun was belt fed, the string of bullets being fed through the gun from a box of ammunition on the floor.

Willy snuck up on the ammo box and lifted it up, tossing it out the doorway of the control room. It fell, its weight snatching the big weapon from Packer's hands and to the rocky ground below. Packer's head snapped around and he snarled as he saw the mechanic in the doorway.

"You again, huh?" He balled his meaty hands into fists. "I'm gonna finish what we started back on the Flying Platform." He charged, knowing for sure the smaller man could never survive the full brunt of his assault.

Willy stood his ground for a split-second. Just before collision, he ducked and darted to the side. Packer suddenly found his charge and his swinging fist passing through empty air. His momentum carried him out the door. Packer's hand swung out and he gripped the doorway, his other hand and his feet trying to find purchase on the ladder as he dangled.

Willy straightened up and faced the dangling thug. "Damn, you're stupid," he said. "You fell for the same thing back on F.P. 1."

Packer grunted. "Aw, to hell with you!" he snarled as he drew a pistol from his belt with his free hand and aimed at Willy.

Even though he was older than his comrades, Willy's best attribute in a fight was his speed. His foot kicked out, a lightning bolt that connected with Packer's gripping hand at the doorway. Broken, the fingers slipped loose and the muscle-bound thug dropped from the doorway and down the sixty foot drop to the ground below.

"You first," Willy grunted under his breath as he turned to the control panel. Among the various lighting and electrical controls, he found the levers that controlled the massive cavern doors. Throwing the switches, he was rewarded with a warning alarm, followed by the sight of dim sunlight as the doors slid open at the end of the cavern. The way to freedom was open, and Willy riddled the controls with bullets. The sudden, brief shower of electrical sparks was his assurance that the doors could not be closed again.

"Diana!"

The aviatrix's head spun when she heard the sound of the familiar voice calling her name. Coming down the ramp from a nearby tunnel mouth, a group of bedraggled looking scientists was moving her way. Several held Tommy guns at the ready for their defense, but Diana's eyes were drawn to the face of Herbert Chalmers in the center of the group. His skin was grey and ashen but his expression bright; here, in the middle of so much violence and evil intent, was the familiar and beautiful face of the woman he had loved. There was still something there in her eyes, and he knew instantly that his work would take a backseat to this woman from here on in. How could he have been so blind to ignore her?

Diana ran to Chalmers and they embraced, fiercely but tenderly. The wounded scientist winced, and Diana helped to support him. "It's okay," she told him, "I'm here now. We're getting out of here." Weakly, Chalmers smiled back and he kissed her passionately.

There was a sudden tremor beneath their feet, a rumble that shook the foundations of the island. A shower of rocks and dust rained down upon the entire facility and the group halted in their tracks.

"What the hell was that?" Diana asked hoarsely as the tremor died to a dull vibration in the ground.

"The Seismic Hammer test," the white bearded scientist that had been stopped earlier by Storm replied. His face was grave. "I tried to tell him but he wouldn't let me go back. The timed test has activated, but the proper safeguards aren't in place. The Hammer is going to tear the island apart."

"We have to go back, turn it off…" Herbert began.

The scientist stopped him with a shake of his head. "It's too far, we'll never make it and we'll be buried or drowned by the time we'd get there."

Diana started walking with the group back toward the *Athena*. "Then we'll just have to get out before the roof falls in," she said in determination. "Come on, let's keep moving."

The group caught up with the other escapees as the last of the captives were being loaded into the *Athena*. As they approached the sub, another tremor rose up and the walls of the stone cavern shook. Boulders broke loose and began rolling into the water or crashing down onto the docks. One of the walls crumbled and took a steel catwalk with it into the black water of the cavern.

Willy ran to the group, out of breath and panting. "Have any of you seen Cliff and Brock?" he asked. "Something's happening to this place and we need to get the hell out of here before it buries us."

"Wait for us!" a voice called. They turned and saw Brock trotting their way across a catwalk that spanned the water. "I think we've overstayed our welcome."

"Where's the boss?" one of the *Independence*'s crewmen asked.

Diana ran to Chalmers and they embraced.

Brock jerked his thumb over his shoulder as he reached the ground at the end of the catwalk. "Behind me." Across the cavern, Storm was beginning to cross the catwalk.

Suddenly, something splashed up out of the water beside the catwalk. It soared up into the air in an arc before it landed with a loud "*clang!*" right in front of the sprinting adventurer. He skidded to a halt before it.

A towering, black steel form stood before Storm on the metal walkway: Poseidon. Manton was defiant to the very end, here in the crumbling seat of his rule, wearing the diving armor he had worn into battle so many times before in his piracy. Sheathed on Manton's back was his water spear weapon. Inside the steel helmet, decorated with its ridge of thorny spikes that represented a crown, Manton glared down at Clifton Storm in rage and fury.

"My kingdom dies today," his voice boomed over the suit's amplifiers, "but so do you."

CHAPTER 24:
THE FURY OF POSEIDON

To the onlookers, the two figures seemed framed there upon the narrow railed platform and time seemed to stand still for a moment. The armored figure of Poseidon towered over Clifton Storm; the adventurer, normally a dynamic and striking individual, was clad in ripped and dirty clothes, clutching only a Colt 1911 automatic for a weapon. Compared with the hulking nemesis before him, Storm seemed small but defiant.

Brock and Willy began to sprint back across the catwalk toward Poseidon's armored back but another thunderous tremor shook the cavern base. Each quake from the Seismic Hammer had been increasing in strength, and this was the strongest yet. It caused the ground to tremble, and a huge chunk of the stone ceiling broke free and dropped down. Rocks and debris smashed through the catwalk behind the villain's back and created a wide gap. Brock and Willy were cut off from their boss. He was on his own.

"We gotta get a gun, something big to get through that damned armor," Brock blurted as he wheeled around to look for a weapon.

"No!" Storm commanded ,his eyes still locked with Manton's hateful gaze within the armor's helmet. "Get the hell out of here and get those captives to safety."

Grudgingly, Storm's friends realized that he was right: the entire island was coming down around them. If they stayed behind any longer they risked killing everyone they had come to save, and it all would have been for nothing. The *Athena* was ready to sail, and Storm's allies and the final group loaded aboard the craft. The futuristic submarine began to move, gliding through the cavern and into the tunnel beyond. The craft reached a bend in the tunnel, and from the deck, the band of adventurers took a last look at their friend and leader as they disappeared from sight. They had just gotten him back, and now they were going to lose him again.

"I'm going to kill you," Manton said, and he lunged forward. He swung a fist with the enhanced power of the armor. Storm leaped back as the fist shot past him, throwing Manton off balance. The punch made a hole in the steel catwalk where Storm had been only a moment before.

Taking a chance, Storm swung up his pistol and fired point blank at the glass visor of Manton's helmet. The bullet merely made a crack in the thick reinforced glass and bounced off. Before he could try another shot, Manton's fist swung in a backhanded strike. The swing struck Storm's forearm and knocked the .45 from his numbed fingers. The pistol sailed through the air and landed in the black water.

In his helmet, Poseidon grinned bloodthirstily and threw another punch. Storm ducked it and shot out his hand in an attempt to grab some of the armor's exposed hydraulic tubing. His fingers found the tubing and he began to tug it, hoping whatever he pulled would slow down the armor in some way.

Manton twisted and grabbed Storm with a growl and threw him as though he was a rag doll. Storm flew through the air and landed on a damp sandbar about fifteen feet away. His body and his head ringing, Storm pushed himself up onto his hands and knees and shook his head in an effort to clear it. Poseidon leaped.

A brief shadow passed between Storm and one of the cavern's overhead lights, and he rolled instinctively just as Poseidon landed where his head had lain only a split-second before. As Storm rolled, Manton reached behind his back and drew his water spear from its holster. Poseidon's personalized weapon, reflecting that of the Greek sea god himself, was shaped like a trident and ended with three prong-shaped barrels instead of one.

Moving swiftly over to where Storm was attempting to rise, Poseidon raised his trident above his head with both hands and stabbed downward. Storm rolled to his right as the prongs came down and embedded in the moist sand where his head had been. Poseidon raised his trident again and Storm jerked out of the way as another strike came down toward his face. Three more times Manton attempted to skewer his opponent, and each time he ended up stabbing only the wet sand.

Enraged and possessed by a fierce bloodlust, Poseidon raised his armored foot; he meant to hold Storm down by the throat as he stabbed the adventurer with his water spear. Storm grabbed the foot with both hands and pushed hard. Caught off balance, Manton toppled backward and onto the sandbar.

Rising to his feet, Storm backed up. He had no weapon, nothing with which to defend himself. As Poseidon attempted to get up, another seismic tremor shook his lair. Both men found it hard to stand and they both toppled over as rocks and pieces of the cavern and its base fell around them. The mouth of the tunnel through which the Athena had left collapsed,, closing off the way out. A large bank of the overhead lights went out with a shower of sparks, sending much of the cavern into near darkness.

"Manton," Storm addressed the madman as he got to his feet again, "This house of cards is coming down around our ears. We need to take this outside or we'll both wind up dead."

"As it should be!" his enemy thundered back. "I would gladly die with my hand around your throat. You took everything from me, at the verge of my conquest. *I was a GOD!*" Leaping to his feet, Poseidon aimed his trident water spear at Storm and pressed the firing stud.

The result was unexpected.

The prongs of Poseidon's trident, after his unsuccessful attempts to spear his opponent, had become clogged and impacted with wet sand. The enhanced strength of the suit had helped drive the nozzles deeper into the sand than was normally humanly possible. When Manton fired the water spear, the pressure instantly built up behind the thickly impacted sand; built up and *backed up.*

The humped tank on the back of Manton's Poseidon armor exploded. Shreds of steel flew outward in all directions, including forward and into Manton's back. Within his helmet, he screamed in pain and surprise, and a trickle of blood oozed from his mouth.

Storm took his chance. Running forward, Storm leaped into the air and down upon Manton's shoulders. Channeling his energy using a technique he'd learned as part of the mysterious martial art known as *jiu-kudo*, Storm struck the neck seams of Manton's helmet. The seal cracked, the metal dented, and Storm dug his fingers into the seam. Wrenched upward, the steel helmet pulled away from its fastening and Storm threw it away. Manton's head was exposed.

His pain momentarily forgotten, Manton swung up his arms with a roar, his armored hands clenching around Storm's neck. Before the hands could crush Storm's throat the adventurer countered by swinging his own flattened hands together at either side of Manton's neck. The two chopping strikes drove down and landed on either side of the pirate's neck, sending Manton's nerve clusters into a flaming inferno of pain and numbness. Poseidon's arms became limp and Storm drove the heel of his left hand forward and into Manton's face, shattering bone and driving splinters of his skull back into his brain.

Storm drew back for another strike but it was over. Manton's eyes rolled back in their ruined sockets and he fell backwards, collapsing dead upon the sandbar.

Victorious, Storm stood over the body of Roderick Manton, who had seen himself as the living incarnation of Poseidon. The murderous swath of Manton's villainy was at an end, his plans for world terror, blackmail, and extortion had been shattered, and the man himself was no more. Storm raised his head and looked around the darkening cavern. He knew it was only a matter of time before the seismic tremors struck again. There was a growing vibration building up in the ground again. There was no time to get through the ruins and to the destructive weapon, no way out that he could find now. He, too, would die here, he realized. He closed his eyes and began to prepare for his final meditation.

"Hey... hey, boss!" a voice called out.

Snapping open his eyes, Storm looked around. He still seemed alone in the ruins of the cavern.

"Over here!" A light suddenly stabbed out and illuminated him before swinging past him.

Turning his head toward the sound, Storm saw the glow of lights underwater and the spotlight that had swung his way a moment earlier. In the distance, beyond mounds of rubble, the *Squintin' Squid* sat on the surface of the water. Scott waved frantically with both arms at Storm. "C'mon, we gotta get out of here."

Hurrying toward the submarine, Storm scrambled over the debris strewn about the floor of the cavern and leaped into the water. He swam furiously to the submarine, and as soon as he climbed onto the hull Scott set the craft into gear. The *Squid* swung around as Storm climbed inside and dogged the hatch shut, and it began sliding beneath the surface of the water.

Piloting the sub toward the utility tunnel they had used to sneak into the base before, Scott said to Storm, "I stuck around for a while in case I was needed but nobody came back for me. From where I was I couldn't see you and Poseidon, so when I saw the big sub leave with the others I left through the access tunnel. I got a call on the radio just as I got back outside: it was from Diana and she said you were still in here with that nut job."

"So you turned around for me?" Storm asked, wiping water from his face.

"Yep. I'm just sorry I showed up so late; I would have loved to have gotten a few licks in on Poseidon too."

Storm grinned at the youth's enthusiasm. "Believe me, you've done quite enough already."

"We're not out yet boss," Scott reminded him. Beyond the *Squid*'s viewports, the tunnel had visibly crumbled. The powerful lights of the little sub illuminated the wreckage around them. Suddenly, the vibrations in the water intensified: another one of the Seismic Hammer's tremors had built and was unleashing itself into the island's foundations. Rocks began falling from the roof of the access tunnel around them, threatening to crush the little craft. Debris bounced noisily against the hull around them.

Ahead of the sub, the opened access vent appeared and Scott pushed the *Squid*'s throttles all the way open. The outline of the tunnel was changing around them as the tremors shook the rocky island apart. It was collapsing behind them.

The *Squintin' Squid* passed through the tunnel's opening into the open sea beyond just before the tunnel's mouth became blocked with a tumbling boulder, three times the size of the little sub. The full throttle escape didn't let up, though: Roderick Manton's lair was crumbling in on itself now, the hollow chambers in the island's foundation giving way. The island was sinking down into the sea, and of its descent threatened to pull them down with it. Massive waves were spreading out from the disintegrating island now, gigantic ripples that were like a last, futile strike from Poseidon's dying hands. The sea became choppy, and as the *Squintin' Squid* neared the surface it was tossed around violently like a cork, shaking the occupants around like nuts in a can.

Within the collapsing walls of Poseidon's lair, the glow of the strange meteorite was suffocated under tons of rock and metal. The strange history of the glowing mass from the depths of space and creation ended here; it sank under rock and seawater along with the machinations and devices of the evil man who had harnessed its mysterious energies.

The Seismic Hammer's power source was finally destroyed under a falling wall of stone, but it was no longer needed: the island was now compromised and sinking itself. With a final shudder, the ruins of the island collapsed completely and began settling upon the floor of the Aegean Sea.

The curse of Poseidon was over.

CHAPTER 25: ON CALMER SEAS

The *Independence* and the *Syracusia* arrived on the scene shortly after the escape of the *Athena*, and no time was wasted: the wounded were taken aboard the MARDL ship where Doc Foster and his staff treated them for their injuries. There had been an estimated one hundred and eighty workers who had been under Poseidon's influence: during the riots and ensuing escape, twenty four of these had been wounded, and thirteen killed. A large number of Manton's pirates had been taken hostage by the workers and Storm's crew also, and many of these were wounded and had given up. Oakley, the rat-faced gangster who'd been one of Manton's right-hand men, had been among those captured, and he would soon be on his way to face his fate at the hands of the authorities, along with Jimmy and several other gangsters who had run afoul of Manton's rage and had been leashed with a meteorite-collar while in his service.

The *Squintin' Squid* rendezvoused with the *Independence,* and the crew was overwhelmed to see Storm and Scott's safe return. In the space of a few short years, the Miami Aerodrome Research and Development Laboratories had grown into a somewhat large but tight-knit family, and they worried for the safety of one and all, especially their leader and founder. Storm's safe return to his fellows was cause for celebration, and once proper arrangements had been made, the crew relaxed and reflected on what had been their most trying adventure yet.

Clifton Storm and his closest aides, however, did not take part in the relaxation just yet. There was still the matter of little Nikos, the only survivor of the attack on Katsopolis and the only reason why Storm was able to facilitate the captives' escape. Orphaned, the boy was without his mother and father now, and would have to be relocated to live with other relatives.

Storm, Brock, Diana, and Willy flew Nikos back to Greece (an exciting event for Nikos, who had never dreamed he would fly in an airplane), where they assisted in the adoption proceedings and eventually took the boy to live with his favorite uncle and aunt, a sweet couple who had their own olive vineyard.

When the time came to say their final goodbyes, Nikos was saddened at their farewell, but Storm delighted the boy by making him an honorary member of MARDL. The troubleshooter made a promise to write to Nikos, and it was a promise the two of them would keep for long afterward.

After saying goodbye to their friends and allies from Greece, the *Independence* set sail back to Miami—the repairs they had made after the fight with Poseidon's forces had been good enough for the time, but a serious overhaul was needed to get the ship back to full operational standards—like an old wounded warrior, the massive super ship was headed back to its home port.

As the *Independence* neared France, a fully-healed Herbert Chalmers and Diana St. Clair announced their engagement to each other. The events of the adventure had drawn them back together, with Chalmers realizing just how much Diana meant to him and Diana realizing that the stable and studiously quiet man was just what she needed to balance out her own adventurous life. Chalmers' wounds were healing just fine, and the two decided to take a celebratory vacation together to see Paris.

In the *Independence*'s launch bay, Chalmers shook Storm's hand warmly as their luggage was being loaded into their plane. "Thanks for everything, Cliff. I owe you my life; I guess all of us that were in those caves do."

Storm smiled back at the bespectacled scientist. "Diana's the one you should really be thanking. She's the one that investigated your disappearance first, on her own. She didn't want to give up and only came to me when her efforts failed. She's one hell of a woman."

Chalmers nodded. "Don't I know it. I'm not letting her get away from me again, not a second time. She wouldn't be able to shake me now, even if she tried. She can keep this adventure stuff, though. It's not for me."

"Nah, you're a man of science; a thinker, not a shooter," Storm replied. "And I hope you'll put those skills to work for me again, Herb. You know you always have a place with us at MARDL."

The other man smiled. "Thanks, boss. I'll think about it and I'll let you know. I can't be sure yet, but keep that spot open. I have a feeling you'll be seeing me there again soon."

"Are we just about ready?" Diana said as she approached the two men. They turned as one and looked at her, and Storm felt the last flickers of what he'd held for her. Diana St. Clair looked stunning in a bright yellow dress and sun hat. The dress was belted with a bright red sash, which mirrored the ruby color of her lips. Her long black tresses framed her face and sapphire eyes, and Storm reflected on just how lucky Herbert Chalmers was.

"Yeah, the crew's just about done getting our things loaded," Chalmers said, looking over the railing and down at the seaplane below. "Hey, watch that stuff, it's fragile!" he called to a crewmember, who was jostling some of Diana's things into the plane. "I've got to go down there and handle those myself. Excuse me," he said to Storm and he raced down the steps to help the crewman load the luggage.

Diana and Storm chuckled, and then turned toward each other. "Listen, Cliff," she began. "I want to tell you something. I know what you feel, toward me I mean."

"I don't..." he started to say.

"Come on, Cliff. I'm not blind, and I'm not stupid. The way you used to look at me, the way you looked at me back on F.P. 1. I want you to know that I'm flattered."

Storm reddened at this. Look at me, he thought to himself, *the big bad globetrotting hero, braving danger and punishing the wicked and blushing like a twelve year-old in love.*

"I'm flattered," Diana repeated, "But I don't think it'd have worked out between us. You and me, we're crazy for doing the things we do, for putting our lives on the line for people we don't even know halfway around the globe. Crazy and crazy don't mix. That man down there, he's the calm I need, my anchor. He's who I need."

"I know," Storm replied. "And I know you're happy together, but it sure could have been fun." He smiled.

"Yes, it could have been." Diana smiled a beaming grin and shook her head. "You didn't get the girl this time, Challenger Storm, but there's one out there for you. I just know there is. Have you thought about Marie?" she asked.

Storm was taken aback a little. "My secretary? Well, yeah, she's cute and all, but why'd you bring her up?"

Diana grinned again, devilishly. "Well, you know how I said I saw you giving me 'that look?'"

He nodded.

"Well, keep that in mind the next time you're talking to her and you just might catch on."

He looked at her, puzzled, and she laughed.

"For an 'adventure hero,' you sure aren't that observant or that bright sometimes." She shook her head and kissed him on the scars on his left cheek. "Stay good, Cliff, don't ever change."

With that, Diana turned and walked down to the waiting seaplane. Though she was a pilot, she wouldn't be flying this trip herself. One of the *Independence*'s pilots would be taking the couple to Paris and returning with the plane, leaving the two lovers to enjoy each other's company unhindered.

With the preparations finished and the passengers and crew boarded, the seaplane taxied out of the bay doors and out onto the open water, where it took off and glinted in the sun as it turned north. As he watched the plane leave from the platform railing, Storm took out a custom-rolled cigar and lit it, inhaling the rich scent of tobacco and hazelnut. He reflected on what Marie had said about Diana St. Clair back in Miami: "*I know you've heard the phrase 'femme fatale' before, and that's her. She'll get you into all kinds of trouble if you follow her.*"

"Well, she's somebody else's trouble now," he said to himself as he smiled and waved at the departing seaplane.

EPILOGUE: THE MID-OCEAN VISITOR

A little over a week had passed since Diana and Chalmers' departure from the MARDL ship. During that time, Christmas had come and gone, and so had New Year. 1934 had rolled into the world to find the *Independence* still limping along on its journey home, her crew weary and looking forward to a little rest once they reached their home port.

It was late at night. The *Independence* was in the middle of the North Atlantic Ocean after its brief stop for refueling at Flying Platform 1. Storm was up late working within his quarters' lab and workshop when his intercom buzzed. Putting aside the gadgetry upon his work table, Storm toggled the intercom.

"There's been a radio message for you, sir," the voice of Horton, the nighttime radio operator, said from the speaker. "There's a plane heading this way, and someone coming aboard to see you. They're about fifteen minutes out from us now."

Puzzled, Storm checked his watch. "It's almost two o'clock in the morning. Who is it?"

"He wouldn't say, sir," Horton replied, "He only said to tell you 'I told you we'd contact you if we needed to.'"

Storm rolled his eyes. "Couldn't he have thought of a secret password or something?" he said to himself.

"What was that, sir?" Horton asked.

"Nothing, never mind. I'll go down to the launch bay to meet him. Thanks, Horton."

Shutting off his intercom, Storm left his lab and quarters, wondering about the coming visit.

The aircraft was a small, nondescript seaplane, a short-range model that must have been launched from a boat somewhere nearby. The unmarked craft slid into the launch bay and crews tied the plane to the moorings. The pilot got out of the craft and remained aloof, while the single passenger made his way up the stairs to the overlooking platform where Storm waited.

The visitor wore a black fedora and a long black coat and suit, immaculately pressed and free from any lint whatsoever. Beneath the brim of the fedora was a handsome though nondescript face. It was the kind of face you could see a million times and still forget once the face's owner walked away. Around the man's neck was a ridiculously ugly necktie that somehow combined stripes, plaid, and the silhouettes of racehorses together into one singularly offensive pattern.

Storm made a face. "Where do you get these ties from, Agent Matheson? They're awful."

"They're gifts from my wife," the visitor replied.

"Oh, I'm sorry," Storm apologized, "I didn't mean anything."

Matheson waved the comments away. "No, don't be sorry, you're right: they're ugly as sin," he said. "I think she does it on purpose, to keep other women away from me when I'm traveling." He smiled for a moment before telling Storm, "Let's take a walk away from here."

Special Agent Jim Matheson was an operative for a secretive U.S. governmental agency that simply called itself "the Eye." The psychically gifted agent had come to Clifton Storm shortly after the Isle of Blood incident with an offer from his group: they would help to run interference with normal government proceedings and allow Storm's troubleshooters to continue operating their unique services, free from scrutiny and legal restrictions. In exchange for this assistance, Storm and his team would occasionally be asked to undertake missions for the Eye; these missions would usually call for Storm and MARDL's specialized skills and abilities in arenas where the participation of the United States would be less than desirable.

Matheson's presence here, in the middle of nowhere, baffled Storm but obviously signaled that he was needed by the government.

The duo rode the elevator to the main deck, discussing the events surrounding Poseidon's curse. It had made big news back in the states, and Storm was already dreading the press waiting for him back home. Matheson apologized for this: there wasn't much he or his agency could do to keep the tabloids from hounding Storm, not when he was doing larger-than-life deeds such as the foiling of modern day pirates armed with super science and ancient superstition.

On the deck, when the two men were alone, Matheson cleared his throat and began.

"Mr. Storm, I realize that you're seeing me much sooner than you expected."

"You're right," Storm interrupted, resting his forearms on the railing overlooking the dark ocean. "I wasn't planning on seeing you for a while. The way you talked, you weren't going to need our help very often."

Matheson cocked his head and nodded. "Yes, that's true. And we *don't* want to take advantage of our arrangements. We weren't planning to contact you until we were able to follow up on those airship hijackers you took down last year. But all of that has changed now. Something has happened, something that could be very big, and very, very bad for the world."

Intrigued, Storm turned from the railing he'd been leaning on and faced Matheson. "What's going on?"

Matheson paused for a moment, and he looked as though he made some internal decision, something he'd been debating for a while. "Now, I know you may not be exactly receptive to what I'm going to tell you, but I want you to listen to me with an open mind, and to consider every possible angle."

"Go on," Storm said. "I'm listening."

Matheson took a deep breath before he spoke next.

"What do you know about the Miskatonic University's 1930 expedition to Antarctica?"

TO BE CONTINUED...

ABOUT OUR CREATORS:

Michael Wm. Kaluta was born in Guatemala to U.S. citizens. He studied at the Richmond Professional Institute (now Virginia Commonwealth University). Michael is probably best known for his work on the comic book series *Starstruck* and *The Shadow*.

Kaluta's early work included Charlton Comics' *Flash Gordon* and an adaptation of Edgar Rice Burroughs's *Venus* novels for DC. Kaluta's influences and style are drawn from pulp illustrations of the 1930s and the turn of the century poster work of Alphonse Mucha rather than the silver age comics of the 1960s. Associated during the 1970s with Bernie Wrightson and Jeffrey Jones he also contributed illustrations to Ted White's *Fantastic* and *Amazing*. He co-created *Eve*, the horror host turned *The Sandman* supporting character.

Kaluta was one of the four comic book artists/fine illustrators/painters who formed the artists' commune The Studio in a loft in Manhattan's Chelsea district from 1975 to 1979 with Barry Windsor-Smith, Jeffrey Jones, and Bernie Wrightson. Aside from many comic books and covers, Kaluta has done a wide variety of book illustrations.

In 1984, he not only drew the illustrations for but directed the music video of The Alan Parsons Project song *Don't Answer Me,* which became one of the most requested videos of the year on cable video channel *MTV.*

Among music fans, Kaluta is known as the artist for the cover of Glenn Danzig's instrumental album *Black Aria* and for the interior illustration of Danzig's fourth album, the latter of which appeared in 1994 and 1995 as a pendant sold at Danzig concerts, and on Danzig T-shirts and sweaters produced in the same period. Kaluta also created the CD covers and interior booklet illustrations for *Nativity in Black I* and *II*, tribute albums to the music of Black Sabbath.

Kaluta has also worked for role-playing game companies such as White Wolf. He has done artwork for collectible card games companies, including a comic book for Wizards of the Coast's *Magic: The Gathering* and illustrating cards on Last Unicorn Games' *Heresy: Kingdom Come.*

His work has won him a good deal of recognition, including the Shazam Award for Outstanding New Talent in 1971 and the 2003 Spectrum Grandmaster Award.

Don Gates is a native of Florida, something of a rarity in the Sunshine State. Born in 1974, he has worked for a toy store and a bakery, worked in a trophy shop and with the developmentally disabled, and has worked customer service from magazine subscriptions to home-phone service. He is married to a loving and feisty wife and the pair has seven "children": 4 dogs, 3 cats. Gates recently moved to Canada and is learning to deal with the weather, which is often a far cry from that of Florida. *The Curse of Poseidon* is Gates' second novel of what he hopes will be many more featuring troubleshooting adventurer Clifton "Challenger" Storm.

Where it all started...

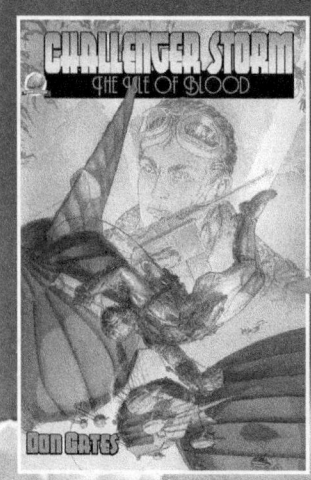

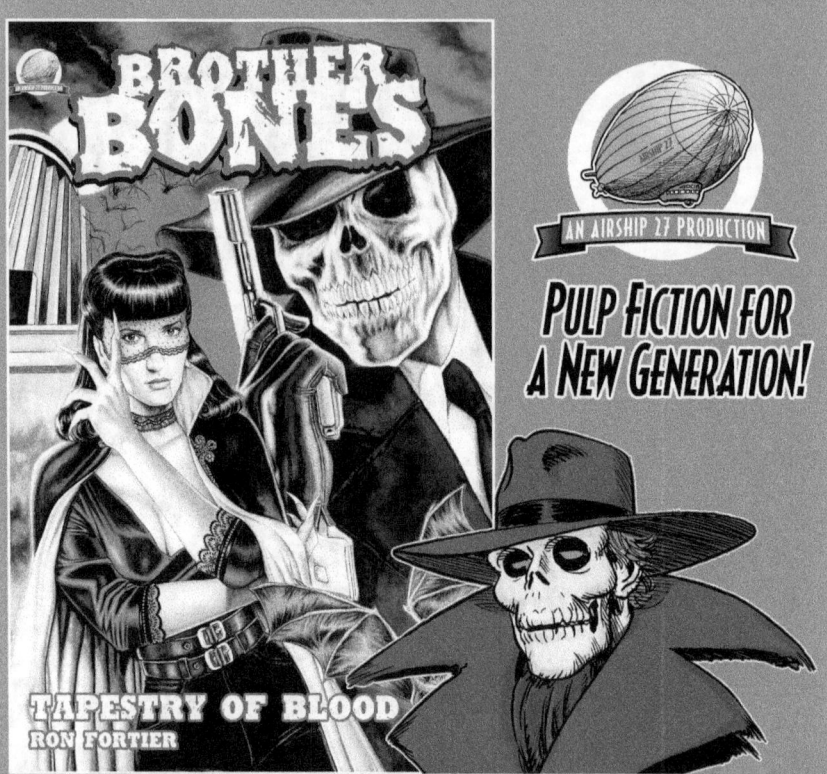

BROTHER BONES

AN AIRSHIP 27 PRODUCTION

PULP FICTION FOR A NEW GENERATION!

TAPESTRY OF BLOOD
RON FORTIER

WELCOME TO CAPE NOIRE

Located on the Northwest Coast, Cape Noire is a booming economic giant whose inner core has been corrupted by all manner of evil. From the sadistic mob bosses who ruthlessly control vast criminal empires to the fiendish creatures that haunt its maze of back alleys, Cape Noire is a modern Babylon of sin and depravity.

Amidst this den of iniquity strides a macabre warrior committed to avenging the innocent and holding back the tide of villainy. He is *Brother Bones, the Undead Avenger* and there is no other like him. A one-time heartless killer, he is now the spirit of vengeance trapped in an undying body. He is the unrelenting sword of justice as meted out by his twin .45 automatics

His face, hidden forever behind an ivory white skull mask, is the entrance to madness for those unfortunate enough to behold it. This new collection features five suspenseful, fast-paced, action-packed stories featuring pulp fiction's most original hero, Brother Bones. Time to draw the shades, light the candles and enter into a Tapestry of Blood!

FOR AVAILABILITY OF THIS AND OTHER FINE PUBLICATIONS CHECK THE WEBSITE: AIRSHIP27HANGAR.COM

www.ingramcontent.com/pod-product-compliance
Lightning Source LLC
Chambersburg PA
CBHW052033260626
47163CB00006B/286